Mine to Keep

Pine Ridge Pack:
Book 2

Jayda Marx

Author's Note

Thank you for your interest in my book! This paranormal romance features my take on some seriously sexy wolf shifters. They share many attributes of shifters found in other fictional works, but not all. This book contains fated mates, steamy moments and lots of laughs. My stories are low angst, **insta-love**, and filled with teeth tingling sweetness! They feature **relationships on the fast track.** I want my readers to finish my books with a smile on their face and a fierce case of the warm and fuzzies. Laughter is guaranteed, and each read delivers its own type of drama. Thanks again for taking a look and happy reading!

Chapter One

Rowan

"What is Dax's favorite color?" I asked Rory, who sat next to me in the middle row of the pack's SUV. We traded in our old truck and Rory's car for a vehicle with third-row seating since our pack was growing. I hoped it'd be growing by one more very soon.

"Here we go again," Stone grumbled from the passenger seat.

I discovered Rory's best friend Dax was my mate about a week ago when I caught his scent lingering on Rory's and Phoenix's skin. Since then, I'd been asking Rory multitudes of questions, desperate for any information I could get about the man whom I was destined to love and protect forever. Rory didn't seem to mind one bit, but Stone wasn't shy about the fact that I was driving him crazy.

"Blue," Rory answered with a gentle smile.

"What shade?"

Stone turned around to give me an unimpressed stare. "Are you serious right now?"

Phoenix chuckled from the driver's seat. "Stone, you'll understand the obsession when you meet your own mate."

"I'm not sure I *want* to meet him if it's gonna turn me all 'pancakes and glitter'."

Rory squinted his eyes. "Who the hell says 'pancakes and glitter'? Usually it's like 'rainbows and unicorns' or something."

"Unicorns aren't real," Stone shrugged.

"Says the man who can turn into a wolf," Rory smirked, making Phoenix chuckle again.

"You tell him, sweetheart."

Stone rolled his eyes and turned forward in his seat again. "Oh thank god, we're here," he said as Phoenix parked the vehicle. He and the Alpha exited, but Rory put his hand on mine, keeping me in place.

"Light blue," he smiled, "Like your eyes."

I let out a happy sigh. "Thank you."

He patted my hand before removing his. "No problem. And don't pay any attention to Stone; he'll be just as lovestruck as the rest of us one of these days, and then you can rub it in his face." I laughed as he pulled his phone out of his pocket. "Wanna see his picture again?"

"Yes!" Rory snorted as I grabbed his cell out of his hand. I pulled up the photo gallery and grinned as I swiped through pictures of Dax. Rory offered to send me some, but I worried it'd be disrespectful to have Dax's picture without his knowledge. That didn't keep me from drooling over the ones Rory had, though. "He's beautiful," I said for the millionth time.

But it was an understatement. Every time I saw his image, it took my breath away. His eyes were the color of melted chocolate and danced with humor. I loved the way they nearly disappeared in the photos where he appeared to be laughing; the way his face lit up with joy. The dark-auburn color of his hair was warm and inviting. I'd fantasized countless times about how his bearded cheeks would feel against my smooth ones; how his gorgeous, soft body would feel in my arms while we snuggled under a blanket.

"Do you think he'll like me?" I asked Rory hopefully. For as long as I'd been looking forward to our meeting, I'd also been worrying about it. Dax was coming over later for a pizza and movie night, and now that the day had arrived, I was more nervous than ever.

"He'll love you," Rory insisted. "You are kind, thoughtful, and caring; all of the things Dax deserves, but has never had."

That was another reason for my anxiety; Dax was already in a relationship with someone else. Rory hated the guy *Justin*; hell, I hated him too for the way I'd heard he treated my mate, but Dax seemed attached. And as much as I wanted him as my own, I couldn't step in the way of Dax's happiness. All I could do was meet him and let him decide. If he rejected me, it'd bring on pain and misery like I'd never experienced, but I had to take the risk.

"Come on," Rory said, patting my leg, "Let's take care of business here and then go home to get ready for his visit. Everything will be okay."

"Thanks, Roar." He smiled and we both climbed out of the vehicle.

Rory stepped next to Phoenix and took his hand. "So this is where you grew up?"

"This is the place." We all took a long look around at the dozens of cabins which now stood abandoned. "But it wasn't like this."

"What do you mean?"

"This used to be a happy place." Phoenix released a long sigh. "When my father controlled these packlands, everyone was taken care of. He was so well respected because he looked out for his people. In turn, we all looked out for each other as well. We all felt safe here. Mothers let their kids shift into pup form and explore on their own because they knew dozens of eyes would be on them, ensuring their safety."

"It was always bustling," Phoenix continued. "With neighbors visiting, pups playing, groups getting together to shift and run through the woods to stretch their legs...now look at it."

Once prized, now the cabins showed age and neglect. Windows were busted out, shutters lay on the ground, and gutters sagged, full of leaves and twigs. Beyond the depressing appearance, the land was veiled in turmoil. The last days of Raven's reign were filled with fear and panic, and those emotions still clung to the air.

"I'm so sorry," Rory told his mate before snuggling into his side. Phoenix wrapped his arms around him and held him close, placing a kiss on the top of Rory's head. Their affections brought a smile to my face; they comforted and supported each other, and their love could be felt by those around them. "But just think; because of you, this will be a happy place again."

After our Alpha defeated his brother in battle, he visited these lands to see if any pack members remained, as he would be *their* new Alpha, but found the place empty just like this. All of Raven's previous members fled to other packs in search of peace. The only ones left were those we fought and killed on our own land.

I supposed that's why he attacked in the first place; to try to grow his dwindling numbers. Or perhaps he was fueled by bloodlust. Maybe it was a last ditch effort to show strength and leadership to his remaining members so that they wouldn't leave him. But his reasons didn't matter now.

We decided as a group that we didn't want to move our pack here. Not only did we like the setup we had for the four of us, we enjoyed our jobs and didn't want to leave. Plus, there were too many negative memories attached to this place, especially for Phoenix. He lost his whole family here.

Instead of giving the lands over to another pack, Phoenix thought it would be best to give the area a fresh start; to let the past lie and bring in new life. So, he donated the land and structures upon it to a local Boy Scout troop. They would hold summer camp here each year, and once things were underway, our pack would volunteer to help the boys learn valuable life skills like survival training, plant and wildlife recognition, and trailblazing. We were all excited to pass along our expertise, and thought it was a great way to honor the memory of Alpha Dean.

Stone clapped his hands together. "Let's get to work."

For hours, Stone, Phoenix and I cleaned and aligned gutters, replaced windows, and rehung shutters with the tools and equipment we brought in the SUV while Rory cleaned the interior of the homes. Most were completely empty, but some had a few lingering pieces of furniture. We left it all for the scouts, unsure what they would need. The troop leader told us he was in the process of getting donations from local businesses, so hopefully by the time summer rolled around, they'd have all they needed. Summer was still several months away, but it was therapeutic for us all to bring the land we grew up in back to its original beauty, and we didn't want to wait.

"This place looks amazing," Rory gushed when we finished, and stood back to admire our work. He took Phoenix's hand and looked into his eyes. "I think your dad would be so proud of you."

"Thank you, sweetheart." Phoenix gave his mate another kiss. "That means so much. I just wish you could have met him."

"He's here in spirit," Stone said with a thump on the Alpha's back, and Phoenix nodded his appreciation.

"There's just one last thing to do," Phoenix said as he turned to me with a gentle smile.

With a nod, I pulled a sage bundle from my pocket, along with a match. I lit the end of the bundle and let it burn for a few seconds before gently blowing out the flame, allowing the tips of the leaves to smolder slowly, releasing thick smoke.

My friends followed me as I walked around and through each cabin, wafting the smoke around and permitting the incense to linger and permeate the air. The sage smudge's purpose was to cleanse the area free of negative energies. Phoenix asked me to perform the act to rid the space of any of Raven's persisting influence. When the process was complete, the air felt lighter and a sense of peace settled over us.

"Thank you, brother," Phoenix told me as he put his hand on my shoulder.

"It was my pleasure."

The four of us smiled as we looked over the homes, now back to their original grandeur. The crowds and laughter were still missing, but they would come.

"Should we get going?" Rory piped up. "Dax is due at our place in just a few hours."

"Yes," I replied quickly. "I need to shower and pick out something nice to wear. I also want to make him a batch of snickerdoodles for his visit, since you told me they were his favorite."

Stone grumbled, "Oh, for fuck's sake," but Rory and Phoenix just gave me wide smiles.

Chapter Two

Dax

Justin shuffled into the bathroom just as I was spritzing myself with cologne, finishing up getting ready for my visit with Rory, his boyfriend Phoenix, and his friends Stone and Rowan. Rory told me all about the other two; I felt like I knew them already, and I was excited to finally meet them.

"So you're really just going to leave me?" he asked, folding his arms across his chest. "You're never home."

"This is the first time I've hung out with Roar in a long time," I insisted. Justin didn't know about the couple of times I'd met him for lunch; one, because I was supposed to be following a diet and what I ate with Rory was *not* on my approved list of foods that Justin gave me. If he knew I cheated, he'd accuse me of not doing my part to try and look nice for him. I *was* trying, but it was hard, and food was really fucking delicious.

I also didn't tell Justin about my meet-ups because he didn't like me spending a lot of time with Rory. He said if I had free time, I should spend it at home doing something useful. Maybe spending time with Rory wasn't 'useful', but for me, it was necessary. He was my best friend and my family and visiting him made me happy.

"I haven't been home much because I'm always at work," I continued. I worked during the afternoon and evenings at the concession stand at the movie theater, and through the night cleaning office buildings. It was hard working two jobs while keeping our house clean and making sure Justin had food prepared in the fridge, but he was between jobs and I did whatever I could to help out.

"Is that a dig at me?" he snarled. "You're at work all the time because I'm a lazy asshole? Because I'm fucking trying."

"I know you are," I insisted, reaching for his hand, but Justin pulled it away. *Shit. I didn't mean to make him upset.* I always seemed to say the wrong thing. "I didn't mean anything by it." His face was still screwed up with anger. "Look, I think we need a night out together. Please, will you come with me?"

"Don't beg, it's embarrassing," he replied with an eye roll. "But no, you just go and talk to all of your little friends about what a loser I am."

"Nobody thinks you're a loser, honeybunch."

"Oh my god, stop with the cutesy nicknames; you know I hate them."

"Sorry." I did know, but sometimes I slipped. Probably because I loved them, but Justin would never give me one. 'Lardass' was as cutesy as it got. I didn't love *it*, but was afraid to point that out since he insisted it was an endearment.

"And since you're running off and leaving me, what the hell am I supposed to eat for dinner?"

"There's leftover lasagna in the fridge."

"So you get fresh, hot food and I get leftovers?"

"It's still fresh; I just made it yesterday between jobs. And if you want fresher, come with me."

"No. Just leave me money and I'll order a pizza."

I pulled a twenty dollar bill from my wallet and handed it over. "I won't be out too late," I promised. I gave him what I hoped was a flirty smile. "Can I get a kiss goodbye?"

Justin huffed and leaned down. My lips barely brushed his cheek before he pulled away. "See you," he said, pulling his phone out of his pocket as he walked towards the living room.

"Bye," I responded, though he was already out of earshot.

I sighed; it'd been weeks since he let me kiss his lips, and months since we'd been intimate. I'd heard that things naturally cool down in relationships over time, but considering we'd been together less than a year, it didn't seem right. Maybe if I followed my diet better and lost a little weight, he'd find me more attractive. Maybe I wasn't doing enough to make him feel valued. Whatever the problem was, I didn't want to pull the plug on our relationship. Especially since it was my *first* relationship. Justin was the first man to ever show me any attention and I was so grateful to him. I'd just have to try harder.

I walked into the living room and sighed again as I grabbed my keys from the hook and left without so much as a glance from Justin.

*****

I followed the directions Rory gave me to find his home. He told me it was in the state forest, but I didn't realize how *in* the forest it was until I turned onto a little dirt service road that led into the trees. I travelled along the winding path until the road dumped onto a clearing where three little wood cabins sat.

The area was adorable and I supposed it made sense that it was within the state park, since Rory's boyfriend and his friends were park rangers of some sort. I wasn't *exactly* sure what they did, but Rory said they looked after the land, maintained the trails and kept hikers safe. The three of them saved my best friend not too long ago, and that was all I really needed to know about them. Anyone to do that was okay in my book, and the way Rory talked about his friends told me they were wonderful guys.

I parked behind a black SUV and stepped out of my little silver car. Just as I shut the door behind me, Rory appeared on the porch of one of the cabins.

"Dax!" He ran full speed at me and threw his arms around my neck when he reached me, nearly knocking me over. I was about an inch taller than him at five foot eight, and quite a bit thicker than him, but not at all stronger. "I'm so happy you're here!"

"Hey, Roar." I wrapped my arms around his slim waist and gave him a good squeeze. "I missed you." It hadn't been that long since I saw him, but I *did* still miss him. We used to live together and saw each other every day, and even though it'd been months, I was still adjusting to daily life without him.

"No Justin?" he asked, looking through my car's window.

"Not tonight," I replied, and Rory smiled. He'd made it clear in the past that he would never be president of Justin's fan club. Rory claimed that my boyfriend didn't treat me right and that I deserved better, but what he didn't understand was that there wasn't exactly a line around my block of men wanting to date me. Plus, Justin had a special place in my heart as my first love. After Rory's opinion caused several arguments between us, he said he just wanted me to be happy and agreed not to mention it anymore.

"Okay, well, the rest of the gang is inside." He took my hand and led me onto the porch of his home. Before he opened the door, he straightened the collar of my button-down plaid shirt and ran his fingers through my hair.

"What are you doing?" I asked with a chuckle.

"Hmm? Oh, nothing." He took a deep breath before gripping the doorknob and giving me a wide smile. "Ready?" He was acting weird, but I figured he was just excited for me to meet his friends.

I nodded and he pushed open the door. The first person I saw was Phoenix, who stepped forward and extended his hand. "It's nice to see you again, Dax."

"It's nice to see you again too." I shook his hand and looked around at the cozy interior of their cabin. Everything looked handmade, and it was full of rustic decor and green accents. "Your place is gorgeous. Thanks for having me over."

"You're always welcome here," he replied with a smile. Then Phoenix let go of my hand and snuggled up next to Rory. Things certainly hadn't seemed to cool off between the two of them; they were constantly all over each other.

"Guys, this is my best friend Dax," Rory announced. "Dax, this is Stone," he said as a huge man stepped in front of me. I thought Phoenix was a muscular guy, but *damn.* Stone was built like a freaking brick wall.

"Good to meet you," he said, holding out a giant hand.

"You too," I greeted. I meant it; it was always nice not being the heaviest guy in the room. Granted my weight was all belly and man boob and Stone's was steel pecs and cast iron abs, but still.

Stone shook my hand in a vise grip and gave me a lopsided smile. "I'm sorry to run out, but it's my shift to check the trails. I'll be back in time for dinner. I just wanted to meet you before I headed out."

"Thanks," I replied with a smile of my own. "It was nice-"

"And *this* is Rowan," Rory interrupted excitedly. I wondered what had him all worked up until another man stepped into my line of vision.

Holy shit. Rowan was one tall drink of water and I was suddenly very thirsty. He was the hottest man I'd ever seen in my life; his jawline was chiseled and smooth, he had soft, dark brown hair and the prettiest ice blue eyes I'd ever seen. He could be a goddamn model. He wasn't as stacked as Stone, but he was just as tall and towered over me.

"It's an honor to finally meet you," he greeted with a dazzling smile. He picked up my hand, which had suddenly gone stupid and limp at my side, and pressed a gentle kiss to my knuckles. A weird gurgling whine crossed my lips. *Smooth.*

When he dropped his hand, I noticed the way his firm muscles shifted beneath his clothes. *God, I'd love a peek beneath those clothes.* I mentally kicked myself for the thought; I was a taken man. I shouldn't be having thoughts like this. *Dax, he's a work of art; it'd be wrong* not *to look! Good point. No, looking leads to touching, and he's off limits. Please, like he'd ever let you touch him, ya human meatball. Stop arguing with yourself and say something!*

"I'm Dax," I replied dumbly. "Well, I guess he already said that. Rory, I mean.

He's my friend. My best friend. Oh, I guess he already said that too." *For the love of Little Debbie, shut the hell up!* This sexy guy had me all kinds of tongue tied.

Thankfully, Rowan didn't look at me like the idiot I undoubtedly was. Instead, his pearly smile just widened. "Absolutely charming."

"Charming? *Me*?" Rowan nodded and that weird gurgle came out of me again.

Stone snorted a laugh. "I hate to miss this show, but I really do have to get going. I'll be back soon." He mumbled something I couldn't quite make out as he left. I think it had something to do with glitter, but I'm *positive* he mentioned pancakes. My ears always pick up the important things.

"We better get going too," Rory said to Phoenix, who nodded his agreement.

"What? Where are you going?"

"To pick up the pizzas," my bestie explained. "The delivery guy won't come up the service road, so we have to meet him down by the park entrance. You and Row hang out here; we won't be long." He practically skipped out of the door, leaving me blinking at the wood when it shut behind him.

"I haven't seen the guy in like a week and he can't wait to leave me," I pouted, propping my hands on my hips. "But since there's pizza involved, I guess I can forgive him."

Rowan chuckled from behind me. "Would you like to join me on the sofa?"

"Oh...um, sure." I turned around and was reminded again of just how ridiculously good looking Rowan was. He definitely got more than his fair share of handsome genes. Rowan motioned to the couch, allowing me to take a seat first. I sat on the right cushion and as he settled in next to me, I said a little prayer that the sofa supported us both.

"It really is wonderful to meet you, Dax," he smiled. "Rory has told me so much about you."

"You too. I actually wanted to thank you for taking such good care of him. Rory told me about how the three of you saved him, and all the teas and cream you made to help him." I put my hand on his, and could've sworn I heard a little gasp escape him. "The words aren't enough, but thank you. I don't know what I would've done without Roar. He's my family."

Rowan put his other hand on top of mine and his large palm warmed my skin. He smiled gently. "I've grown very close to Rory over the past several weeks. He's my family as well, and it was my pleasure to help him."

I smiled back at him; Rory told me how sweet and genuine the guy was, and I could hear it in his words and feel it in his touch. *Shit*. I realized he still had my hand sandwiched, and I pulled my fingers free. It wasn't that he made me uncomfortable; just the opposite. I liked the warmth and softness of his hand on mine, and that was a problem.

"So, where did you learn all of your..." *What did Roar call it again?* "Healing?"

"Before I moved here with Phoenix and Stone, I spent a lot of time with another natural healer named Tessa. She taught me everything she knew about the healing properties of plants and herbal remedies. Plus, I love reading every book I can find on the subject. I'm fascinated by all of the things nature can give us." His cheeks pinked. "I know that makes me sound kinda nerdy."

"Not at all," I insisted. "I think it's awesome. It's a shame more people don't know about that kind of stuff. I always wanted to learn about it; I wanted to be a Boy Scout when I was younger to learn all that cool shit like building fires and knowing what kinds of berries to eat on a hike. Well, to be honest, I was more excited about the berries than the hike."

Rowan's pretty eyes twinkled when he smiled. "So why didn't you join the scouts?"

"My parents wouldn't let their fag son join a group 'just so he could suck dick all the time'."

"Jesus, Dax," he replied, dragging a hand down his face. *Oops*. Guess he wasn't ready for that. Probably wouldn't be ready for this either.

"Plus, the other boys weren't too keen on having a fag trying to suck their dick." I rolled my eyes. "I got beat up a lot for that request, when I didn't care about *anyone's* dick. I just wanted to learn how to build a damn fire."

"I'm so sorry," he replied quietly, putting his hand on mine again. His touch soothed away the sting of the memory. "People can be so small minded. They fear what they don't understand." I nodded my agreement and gave him a tight smile. "You know, it's kind of funny that you mentioned Boy Scouts. I was just at what will be a summer camp earlier today."

When I tipped my head in confusion, Rowan told me all about working to make a camp from old abandoned cabins. My heart melted; the man was so kind to volunteer his time to not only build a place for kids to go, but also to teach them there. He was pretty incredible.

"That's so cool," I smiled when he finished with his story.

"I know it's not the same and tell me if you think it's stupid, but I'd love to teach you how to build a fire and scavenge and everything else you'd like to learn."

"Seriously?" *Yep, pretty incredible.*

"Sure. I'm teaching Rory too and he's really enjoying it."

"That sounds great, thank you. Although, my work schedule is kind of crazy and I don't know how often I can get up here." Rowan's eyes flickered with what looked like sadness, and then it was gone. I was probably imagining things. "But let's have a cram session; what's the number one thing I need to know? Like, what's the best, most useful plant out there?"

"No pressure or anything," he teased with a wink, and my smile widened. "Okay, if I had to pick *one* plant that dominates the rest, I'd go with...cinnamon."

"Really?" I asked in surprise. "I wasn't expecting that. I thought you'd say like some rare, exotic flower from the Aleutian Islands or something."

"Oh shoot, I forgot about that one," he replied, snapping his fingers.

I blinked at him. "Are...are you being serious?" Rowan laughed out loud and I shoved him playfully on the shoulder. "Ha, ha, very funny," I said with an eye roll, although it *was* pretty funny. I loved sarcasm and playful teasing.

"I'm sorry," he smiled with a squeeze to my hand. I was so comfortable with his hand on mine, I'd forgotten it was there.

"Yeah, yeah. So let's hear about what makes cinnamon so much better than my exotic flower."

Rowan chuckled again. "Well, cinnamon has lots of antioxidants, has anti-inflammatory properties, can help manage blood sugar, and can help fight fungal infections."

"Well hot damn, I eat Cinnamon Toast Crunch like every day! I'm probably damn near bulletproof by now."

Rowan tipped his head back and laughed. The deep, warm sound made my stomach flip. "I love your sense of humor." *At least someone does.* Justin always called my dumb jokes immature and embarrassing. *Shit, Justin.* My stomach stopped flipping and knotted up in guilt. I once again pulled my hand free of Rowan's.

"So…" I searched my mind for another question. "You told me the *best* plant, but what's your *favorite* plant?"

"Like my favorite flower?" I nodded. "Hmm...I think you should try to guess."

"Okay, I'm down with that." I was a little competitive, even about things that didn't matter. I wanted to guess correctly. I tapped my chin as I studied him. "Roses." *Everybody loves roses.*

"I like roses, but they're not my favorite."

Damn. "Okay then...daisies."

"Getting closer."

"Yes!" Rowan chuckled at my excitement. "I'm thinking...lilies." He shook his head no. "Well, shit. What is it?"

"I may have cheated a little; I don't have one particular favorite." My jaw dropped and Rowan laughed before explaining, "I've always been drawn to wildflowers. They're strong and can thrive in tough conditions. People often overlook them because they're different or imperfect, but I think that makes them even more beautiful."

My heart sped up as I looked into his enchanting eyes; something told me he was talking about more than wildflowers. Or maybe I just *hoped* he was. Either way, it took all of my willpower to tear my gaze away from him.

"So, um," I cleared my throat to steady my voice. "What movie are we watching tonight?"

It took Rowan a moment to answer, "I'm not sure. Rory vetoed my pick of a horror film."

"I love scary movies too," I smiled. "But I'm not surprised Rory said no. He hates them."

"He told me about making you sleep in bed with him for a week after watching *It* together at your old place," he replied with a laugh.

"Did he tell you about how he made me check his closest for a month after watching *Boogeyman*?"

He chuckled harder. "No, but that was a good movie; so underrated."

"Right? Suspense is the best kind of horror."

We fell into easy conversation and discovered we had so many things in common; from simple things like our favorite color (blue) to important things like our favorite movie (*Identity*) and favorite dessert (cherry cheesecake). And yes, dessert is *very* important.

All of our talk about food must have perked up my stomach, because it gave a long, angry-sounding growl. "Sorry." I ducked my head with embarrassment at the loud sound. "I guess I'm really ready for that pizza."

"Oh, that reminds me; I made something for you." Rowan stood from the sofa and hurried into the kitchen. He returned carrying a plate piled high with snickerdoodles. "Rory told me they were your favorite."

I took the platter with wide eyes. "You made these for *me*?" Rowan nodded with a smile as he sat beside me again. My heart swelled; besides Rory, no one had ever done something so sweet for me.

Sure, it was just a plate of cookies, but to me, it was so much more; he made them for *me*, just because he thought I'd like them. He noticed that I was hungry and instead of making fun of me or ordering me to go fix something, he offered me something made by his own hands. He handed me a plate of sweets with no judgement, and without giving a limit as to what I should eat. My chest warmed so much and so quickly that it was alarming. I pressed my hand over my heart, making sure it wasn't beating out of control.

"Are you okay?" Rowan asked with a look of concern. He pressed two fingers to my throat to check my pulse and his palm over my forehead to see if I had a fever. I won't lie; it was nice to be looked after.

"Yeah, I'm fine," I answered with what I hoped was a reassuring smile. "My chest just did this warm flippy thing. It was weird." Rowan's face melted into a dreamy grin and the plate of cookies in my hand was the only thing that could draw my attention away. I picked one up and offered the tray to Rowan. "Will you have one with me?"

"I don't mind if I do." He picked up a treat and tapped it to mine in a 'cheers' motion before taking a bite.

When I bit into my cookie, I couldn't stop the moan that crossed my lips. It was the naughtiest sound my body had made in months. "Oh my god. Row, this is *so* good."

Rowan blinked rapidly and cleared his throat twice before answering, "I'm so glad you like them."

"Mm, I could sit here and eat this entire freaking plate." I licked my fingers clean before setting the platter on the coffee table with a sigh. "But I better stop at one."

"Saving the rest for after dinner?"

"Well...not exactly. See, I'm supposed to be on this diet..." I stopped talking when Rowan's face scrunched up in what looked like a mix of offense and confusion.

"Why?"

I looked down over my round, squishy body. I wasn't obese by any means, but I was definitely packing around an extra forty or fifty pounds I didn't need. I was probably my own biggest critic and saw myself as larger than what I really was, but it should be obvious to anyone that I was overweight.

I peered back at Rowan. "Are you teasing me?"

It was his turn to press a hand on his chest, and the look of hurt that crossed his face threatened to tear me apart. "I would never." He picked up both of my hands and ran his thumbs along the backs of my knuckles. "Dax, I think you are the most beautiful man I've ever laid eyes on."

My first reaction was to scoff or roll my eyes; to take his words as yet another joke at my expense, but I couldn't doubt the sincerity of his voice, or the adoring way he gazed into my eyes. "Even though I'm kind of...you know...fat?"

The same pained expression from earlier crossed his features and my chest ached. I didn't want to cause him anything but happiness. This man I'd known for such a short time had a strange hold on me; I wanted to see him smile. I wanted to do anything in my power to make him happy and keep him from hurting.

Before I could apologize for whatever I said wrong and ask what I could do to make him feel better, Rowan squeezed my hands and said, "Dax, your body is perfect to me; luscious and inviting. I love your soft curves. I love the way your body quakes when you laugh; like you're so full of joy you can't contain it. And it's not just your outsides that are beautiful, but your insides. You are funny and kind and just being near you makes me happy. You're my wildflower.

You are something wonderful to be cherished, and I promise to do everything I can to make you see it."

Rowan released one of my hands to cup my scruffy cheek and a shiver rocked through my body. His touch was gentle and caring, and I craved it; I needed more. I wanted his hands all over me. I wanted to touch his body and feel his strength while curling up in the warmth his sweet words gave me. No one had ever said such beautiful things to me; made me *feel* beautiful. I was greedy for more of his words, his touch, and his presence. My head spun, trying to make sense of it all. It was fast and scary and wonderful. It was wrong but it felt so fucking right. Something inside me was *screaming* that I belonged with this man, but how could it be when I already belonged to another?

My thoughts went silent as Rowan slowly inched his face toward mine. His fingers tenderly brushed over my cheek, combing through my beard. His eyes bore into mine with such intensity and care I couldn't look away. I couldn't fight this, and the thought of doing so brought the ache back in my chest. My breathing quickened and my pulse pounded as we closed in. I was leaning forward too; his lips were magnets to mine.

Just before we kissed, the sound of the front door opening snapped me from my trance. I jumped up from the sofa and my head spun so fiercely I almost fell over. Rowan reached for me, but I swatted him away. *What the hell did I almost do?*

"Is everything okay?" Rory asked cautiously as he stepped inside his home. Phoenix trailed in behind him, carrying enough pizzas to feed twelve people.

I scrubbed a hand through my hair and over my face, trying to settle myself down. "Um, Rory can I...can I talk to you for a minute?" I squeaked out.

"Of course." He pointed to the wall behind me. "My bedroom's through there."

I kept my eyes on the floor as I followed my friend into his bedroom and he shut the door behind us. I flopped onto his bed and buried my face into my hands. Rory sat beside me and wrapped his arm around my shoulders.

"What's wrong?"

"I'm a terrible person," I mumbled into my palms.

"No you're not. You're a great person." He peeled my hands away. "Why would you think differently?"

I let out a long sigh. "I think I kind of maybe have a crush on Rowan."

"Rowan's a good guy," Rory smiled.

"Yes he is. He's nice and funny and I mean, have you *seen* him? It's like someone liquified sex, poured it into a perfect body mold and out popped Rowan." Rory snickered at my nonsensical words. "And my god, Roar..." I sighed again. "He said the sweetest things to me. He told me I was beautiful. No one's ever told me that before!"

"Hey, I've told you that for years," he scowled. I flinched when I heard what sounded like a low growl. "Forest wildlife," Rory explained, narrowing his eyes at the bedroom door. *Weird*. But I had more important things to worry about than the coyotes outside that would surely see me as a giant glazed ham.

"Yeah, but you told me in a 'you're my friend and I want to support you' way." Rory raised his eyebrows. "Which is wonderful and I appreciate it, but Rowan told me in an 'I want you naked' sort of way; a way that made my heart go all flippy and my dick go all stiffy."

Rory laughed again, and there was another growly sound, but this one sounded different. Less irritated and more...throaty? *That sounds like it's right on the other side of the wall.*

"So what's the problem?" Rory asked, drawing my attention away from the noise.

"What's the problem?" I repeated too loudly, jumping from the bed and throwing my hands in the air. "The problem is I'm already dating someone! Justin is sitting at home - *our* home - trusting that I'm not going to go out and mess around on him." I swallowed hard. "And I almost did. I almost kissed him, Roar. I wanted to; god, I wanted to. It's like he was calling out to me; pulling me into him and I wanted to go. I wanted so much with him."

I wiped a hand down my face. "And *that's* why I'm a terrible person. Maybe Justin isn't perfect and I *know* our relationship isn't perfect, but we do still have a relationship. He trusts me and I can't be acting like this. I think I just need to go home and be with Justin right now. I want to spend time with you, but I just can't be around Rowan. He's too big of a temptation and it's not fair to my boyfriend."

Rory gave me a sad smile, but before he could say anything, there was a gentle knock on the door before it opened. Rowan's face appeared, and he looked so much different than he did just a few minutes ago; his skin was pale and his eyes weren't glistening with the same light.

"I'm sorry to interrupt," he said in a strained voice, "But I'm afraid I have to leave. I'm not feeling very well."

"Are you okay?" I asked, stepping closer to him. Rowan gave me an unconvincing smile and nod. He sure didn't *look* okay. I didn't know what could have gotten him so sick so quickly. *It couldn't have been the cookies; I feel fine.* Well, *fine* was a stretch; I felt like shit about *having* feelings for Rowan, and seeing him like this certainly wasn't helping.

"I understand," Rory said, standing from the bed and wrapping his arms around Rowan's waist. Rowan hugged him back and my heart squeezed with jealousy and a fresh round of guilt. I looked away from them before I did something stupid. "Take care of yourself, Row. I'll come around later to check on you."

Rowan gave my friend a forced smile before turning it on me. "It really was an honor to meet you Dax," he said with a slight bow of his head. "I truly hope we'll see each other again." His gaze raked over my body once more before he left the room. I wanted to run after him, but kept my feet still. Not only was he ill and needed his space, I needed to stay away from him. The thought was like a knife to my chest, but I breathed through it.

"Come on," Rory said quietly while rubbing his hand over my back. "Let's go eat."

For the first time in my life, food didn't appeal to me.

*****

Rowan

I staggered back to my own cabin; each step away from my mate was harder than the last. My wolf paced my mind in a huff, demanding I go back to Dax. I wanted nothing more, but I couldn't do it to my perfect man. He needed space and I had to respect that.

I climbed into my bed, too drained to stand any longer. Dax's rejection weakened me and filled my body with pain more intense than what I believed to be possible. Every fiber; every cell in my body cried out in misery over the loss of my mate. What made it worse was knowing he had feelings for me; he wanted me, but he wanted someone else more.

I knew it was a possibility before we met that Dax could turn me down for his boyfriend, but it was a chance I had to take. Not meeting my mate when I knew of his identity would have driven me mad. Though it hurt being apart from him now, I wouldn't trade my time with him for anything. I'd witnessed his caring soul and joyful spirit, and I'd treasure the memories.

I eased my shirt over my head and buried my nose into the fabric, inhaling deeply. Dax's scent was embedded into it and I wanted to enjoy it as long as possible. He smelled of vanilla with a touch of cinnamon, and it captured him perfectly; sweet with a little spice.

All I could do was wait and pray that Dax changed his mind. My body ached and my soul was shattered, but just those few precious moments with Dax were worth it. I'd lie in suffering and try to soothe my troubled soul with mental images of my mate's pretty eyes shrinking into slits as he let out a belly laugh, and the memory of how his skin felt against mine; how my lips tingled with our almost-kiss.

I hoped that my love didn't feel this kind of pain from us being apart, and that if he did, being close to his boyfriend would soothe it away. The thought made my suffering intensify, but I just wanted Dax to be happy.

Chapter Three

Dax

I heaved into the toilet bowl again, but nothing came out. I wasn't surprised I was empty; I'd been vomiting for the past four days, ever since I left Rory's place. I wasn't sure exactly what I had, but I'd never been so sick in my life. I even had to call off work from both of my jobs, which wasn't like me at all. I'd never missed a day before this. *I must have caught whatever illness Rowan had.* Just the thought of the wonderful man made me heave again. Anytime he crossed my mind, which was often, I felt worse. It was almost like my body was sick *for* him, but I knew that was impossible.

I wondered how the sweet man would react if he saw me like this; he flipped his shit when I just pressed a hand to my chest. He'd probably fall all over himself trying to help me if he saw what misery I was in now.

I managed to heave myself off of the floor, rinse my face with cool water and swish some mouthwash. I waddled into the living room, holding my spinning head in my hands. I sat down on the couch next to Justin, who was playing a video game of some kind. He loved video games. He never let me play with him because I was admittedly pretty terrible, but he did let me watch as long as I didn't disturb his focus. When he pressed pause on his game and turned to me, my heart leapt with hope that he was going to console me for being so sick.

"So what's for dinner?" he asked, looking at me in confusion like he was trying to figure out why I wasn't serving his food.

"Is it dinner time? I guess I hadn't realized since I'm not hungry."

"Well there's a goddamn miracle," he replied with an eye roll. I shrugged off his words; I hadn't fed him all afternoon and he was probably getting cranky.

"I'm sorry, but I don't think I can cook. You're going to have to order out again."

"I've been eating take out for almost a week. I want real food."

"I know sweetie, but I'm sick."

"You're lazy. And if you keep missing work, we won't be *able* to order out because we won't have any fucking money. You said you'd cook and clean this place and you haven't been doing either."

"As soon as I'm feeling better, I promise I'll do it."

"You're so selfish. I have to live in filth and eat shitty delivered food because your fat ass is slacking."

Angry words bubbled up my throat, but I swallowed them down. I knew it wouldn't do any good to fight with him. Justin's temper ran hot and if I poked at him, it'd just make things worse. "The house isn't *filthy*," I pointed out, trying to calm him down. "There's just some takeout containers here and there. If you'd just throw them out after you eat, they wouldn't stack up. And if you're tired of delivery, there's still some frozen food I bought at the grocery store last week. You'd just have to put it in the oven."

"You want me to cook and clean like some fucking bitch?" he roared. "Watch your mouth!" Before I knew what was happening, Justin lifted his arm and swung, backhanding me across the face. I pressed my hand against my heated cheek and blinked up at him, completely stunned. "Give me some money. I'm going out." Not wanting things to get worse, I dug my wallet out of my pocket and handed over every dollar I had. "I want this place clean when I get back." Justin stormed out of the house, slamming the door behind him.

My mind whirled as it tried to piece together what just happened. During all the time we'd been together, Justin had never raised a hand towards me. He'd lose his temper and cuss me out or call me names, but I shrugged them off or even told myself I deserved it. Maybe I wasn't perfect, but I sure as fuck didn't deserve to get hit.

I stomped into my bedroom (Justin didn't share a room with me because he said I took up too much bed) feeling stronger than I had all week. I dug a duffel bag out from under my bed and slammed it on the mattress.

"Who the fuck do you think you are, putting your hands on me?" I grumbled into the room as I shoved piles of clothes into my bag. "I should have knocked you right the hell out." It was easy to say now that he wasn't in front of me. Even if I *hadn't* been in utter shock when he struck me, I wouldn't have stood a chance against Justin. He wasn't exactly muscular, but he was stronger than me.

"I don't deserve to get hit," I insisted to myself as I grabbed my toothbrush from the bathroom. "Call me lazy; *you're* fucking lazy. I cook and clean for you while working two jobs to keep this place running and you just sit on your ass playing video games." I was letting out all the things I was too scared to say to Justin's face; all the things that had been festering inside me for nearly a year. I wished my words could soak into the walls and echo back out when Justin got home.

"Rory was right; you treated me like shit. I did *everything* for you and all you did was try to put me on a diet; not for my health, not because you cared, but because you thought I wasn't good enough for you. *Well guess what*?" I shouted into the empty house. "I am good enough! I'm kind and funny and caring and *too* good for you, you abusive piece of shit!"

I zipped my duffel bag and forcefully threw it over my shoulder. "You were abusive before you ever put a finger on me! You called me names and made me feel worthless!" Tears streamed down my face as

I screamed at the top of my lungs. "I'm not fucking worthless!"

I stormed into the living room and something wicked came over me as I looked over all of the takeout containers on the coffee table. I flashed a wild smile and punted each of them onto the floor, spilling sauce and stains onto the carpet. I got sick satisfaction out of imagining Justin on his hands and knees scrubbing them up.

I marched to the door and took one last look around the place. I wouldn't be coming back. I tried making things work with Justin. I tried being the best I could be. But I realized now that *I* was never the problem. Justin never loved me. Love doesn't behave like that.

I'd witnessed love. Love was Phoenix proudly holding Rory in his lap as they watched a movie together. Love was Stone, Phoenix and Rowan saving my best friend and looking after him. Love was Rory calling me every day to check how I was feeling.

Love was making me a plate of snickerdoodles and making sure I had enough to eat. And I deserved love.

"I'm a motherfucking wildflower," I said before slamming the door behind me.

Chapter Four

Rowan

"It's me," Rory called out as he entered my bedroom, even though I was expecting him. He visited at the same time the past four days to bring me dinner, even though I was able to eat very little. "I made your favorite tonight," he said, presenting a plate of spaghetti. "I thought maybe that'd help you get down more than a couple of bites."

"Thanks, Roar," I croaked out in a gravelly voice. It hurt to speak, but I wanted to show my appreciation for my friend. He was infallibly sweet and doing everything he could think of to care for me, even though the only thing that would truly heal me was reconnecting with my mate.

"No problem." Rory scooted a dining room chair that he'd stashed in the corner over to my bedside. He sat down and began chopping up the food into tiny pieces. "Not to brag, but this spaghetti is pretty freaking delicious. Phoenix ate three plates before heading out on patrol. I'm still not used to him leaving right after dinner to hit the trails before dark. Every year it always takes me a few days to get used to the time change." He scooped up a bite and held it to my lips.

I was too weak and sick to even feed myself, but Rory never seemed bothered. He brought me food every day and made it as simple as possible for me to get some down without ever saying a negative word. Stone and Phoenix visited throughout the day as well and helped me to the bathroom since they were the only ones strong enough to lift me. My brothers took care of me without question and I could never thank them enough, and I'd happily do the same for them.

I pried my lips open and Rory dumped the noodle bits onto my tongue. I managed to get out, "Good," before working the food back on my tongue and swallowing it down.

"Thanks. You know, Dax loves spaghetti too. Italian food is his favorite; pizza, spaghetti, fettucini, you name it." I gave him the best smile I could; he always told me things about my mate when he visited, even when I was too weak to ask. "He's always wanted to go to Italy. Maybe the two of you could go one day. Ooh, I know; all five of us should visit together. I can guilt Phoenix into it; I never got a honeymoon since we didn't technically have a wedding. Once you're feeling better, you can help me talk him into it, okay?"

I gave him a little wink. He always kept a positive attitude and tried to keep my spirits up. "Sweet. I'm excited for my gondola ride already." I huffed a laugh and we both blinked in surprise. It was the first one in nearly a week. "Do you think you can eat some more?"

"Yeah," I said in a voice that sounded more like my own. Unbelievably, I felt hungry. I planted my palms on the mattress and pushed myself into a sitting position.

"Holy crap," Rory smiled, his eyes shining behind his glasses, "I knew my pasta was good, but I didn't know it had this kind of power." I laughed again and he fed me another bite. "Do you think you're feeling because we're talking about Dax?"

I shook my head. We (well, mainly Rory) talked about Dax every day he came over and I didn't feel like this. "Only one thing can make me feel stronger." A wide smile crossed my lips. "Dax is coming back."

"I knew it!" Rory scooped up a huge bite and fed it to me. "I told you he'd be back. He just had to meet you and see the difference between you and Justin for himself. Once you've tasted filet mignon, it's hard to go back to ground beef." He scrunched up his nose. "Not that I'd even put Justin in the 'meat' category. It'd be more like going back to pig slop."

I laughed out loud at the silly man at my side. He beamed back at me and tried to feed me another bite, but I gently stopped his hand. "I think I can manage now."

"Oh, right. Sorry," he said, passing over the plate and fork.

"Please don't apologize. Rory, I couldn't have made it through these past few days without you or the others. I appreciate everything you've done for me and I thank you from the bottom of my heart."

"That's what we're here for," he insisted. "We'll always look out for each other. That's what a pack is all about, right?"

"Right."

"Eat up, eat up," he encouraged. "You'll need all of your strength back when Dax comes to get his man." He made his eyebrows dance, and then laughed as I scarfed down the rest of the food on my plate. "I'll go rinse this off in the kitchen while you get some fresh clothes on." I'd been wearing the same outfit for four days straight. As much as Stone and Phoenix cared for me, they were putting off washing my body and changing my clothes until the last possible minute, and I understood.

"I think I'll take a quick shower."

"Good idea," Rory nodded. "I didn't want to say anything, but you're a little ripe."

"Okay then, maybe it won't be so quick." Rory chuckled as he left my bedroom, heading towards the kitchen.

I took a fast (but thorough) shower and dressed in a nice pair of jeans and a light blue sweater, wanting to look good for my mate while sporting his favorite color.

"Aw, you look so nice," Rory complimented when I stepped out of my room. He was waiting in the living room, watching out of the window for his friend to arrive.

"Thanks. Would you like to wait out on the porch with me?" Dusk was settling and the evening was undoubtedly getting cooler, but I didn't mind. It was only a few steps out onto the porch, but it felt like I was getting closer to my mate.

"Sure."

We stepped outside together and leaned on the porch railing. I assumed Rory was like me; too restless to sit down. I didn't take my eyes off of the service road, not wanting to miss the second when Dax arrived.

My heart leapt when I saw his little silver car bouncing down the dirt path. "He's here," I told Rory, though he surely saw since he was right next to me.

"This is so exciting!" he squealed, bouncing on his toes.

When Dax pulled into the clearing, my heart dropped. I could see that his face was pink and puffy. "He's been crying."

"Shit." Rory took off down the stairs, but I was faster. I sped towards my mate's car and opened his door for him. I spotted a packed duffle bag in his passenger seat, and hope and confusion battled inside me.

To my surprise, Dax climbed out of his car and then buried his face into my chest. I wrapped my arms around him and rocked him gently back and forth as he sobbed against me.

"It's okay," I whispered. "It's okay, I've got you." Rory appeared at my side and gave me a puzzled look. I shrugged but didn't move away from my mate. I didn't know what was wrong, but he needed me and I'd always be there for him. "What is it, Dax? What's wrong?" I rubbed my hands up and down his back, trying to soothe him enough so that he could talk to me.

"He...hit...me!" he wailed, squeezing me tighter around my waist. *Oh, fuck no!*

"Oh, fuck no!" Rory yelled beside me. *At least we're in agreement.* "Just wait until Phoenix gets back. He'll drive into town and shove Justin's head right up his asshole!"

"We don't need to wait for Phoenix," I insisted. "I'll do it now." Normally I wouldn't move against anyone without permission from my Alpha, but this involved my mate, so I was within my rights. "Where is he, Dax? Tell me where he is and I swear to you, he'll pay. Nobody touches my-" I stopped myself and swallowed hard. "Nobody touches you."

"No, please don't leave me," Dax begged. "I need you here, okay? Both of you."

"Okay," I answered quietly. "I'm here. I'm not going anywhere." It took all of my resolve to tamp down my bloodlust. But Dax didn't need a macho man to fight his enemies right now; he needed caring words and a loving touch, and that's exactly what I'd give to him. "I'm sorry for getting upset, cookie. I just can't stand the thought of anyone hurting you."

I didn't even realize what I'd called him until Dax cried harder and hiccupped,

"Cutesy nickname." I shot my gaze to Rory for clarity, but he just shrugged his confusion.

I held Dax for a while longer until he settled in my arms. "Do you think you can tell us what happened?"

Dax nodded against my chest and took a step back. Rory gasped and I clenched my fists at the first good look I got at Dax's face. A large, dark red bruise covered his right cheek and it was already starting to blacken under his eye.

"I've been really sick the past few days," Dax began, and my heart dropped. *He felt it too*; the mate pull. His soul was calling out to me as mine was to him, but because we were apart, he experienced pain and illness. I was hoping he wouldn't feel it since he rejected being with me, but that wasn't the case. "I know I don't really look sick now, but I'm telling the truth. I could barely get around and I was so nauseated and weak. It's weird, though; the closer I got to this place, the better I felt."

Oh, sweet Dax. There was so much I needed to tell him, but I didn't want to interrupt his story. "Anyway," he continued, "I was so sick that I couldn't cook or clean and I had to take time off work. Justin got mad and when I suggested he cook for himself, he hit me. Then he left. Then I left and I'm not going back. I'm done with him. If I never see his face again, it'll still be a day too soon."

"Good for you," I told him proudly. Even if he didn't want to be with me, he deserved better than that asshole, and I was happy he finally saw that.

Dax wiped his eyes angrily. "I probably look so pathetic right now." Before I could argue, he added, "But I'm not crying because he hit me or because I miss him or any of that shit. I'm crying because I'm so fucking angry; angry at him for treating me so terribly this whole time, and angry at myself for not listening to you." He nodded his head to Rory. "You tried to tell me that Justin was no good, but I didn't want to hear it. I just wanted a relationship so badly that I let him walk all over me. I should've known you just wanted the best for me and I'm so sorry."

"Dax, no," Rory replied gently, but his friend wasn't done.

"And I'm so mad at myself for staying with him for so long; for letting him treat me like that. I just kept telling myself it would get better and that at least I had someone." He shook his head. "God, I'm such an idiot."

I stepped forward and captured him in my arms again. "You're not an idiot," I insisted. "You stayed with him because you wanted to be loved, which is something everyone wants. You tried seeing the best in him; you assumed there was some good in him because there's so much good in you, but some people are just evil. He's the only one at fault here, Dax. None of this is your fault. I'm so proud of you for standing up for yourself and leaving. You're so strong."

"Thank you," he said in a wobbly voice before stepping back again. "I came here because I knew Rory would let me stay with him-" he paused and smiled at his friend, who was nodding rapidly, "But there was another reason that drew me here." He reached out and took my hand. "I wanted to tell you...oh shit."

Oh shit? He wanted to tell me oh shit? I looked to Rory again, just to find him looking to his left; the same place Dax was looking. The same place where Phoenix stood about fifteen feet in front of us in wolf form, having just come from the woods when he finished his rounds. *Oh shit.*

Dax shocked the hell out of me by jumping in front of both Rory and me and spreading his arms out to the side, as if to shield us from the animal. My heart swelled at his bravery and sacrifice, even though they weren't necessary.

"Get out of here!" he yelled, flapping his hands at Phoenix in a shooing motion. "Go on, get!"

Stone's front door opened and he stepped out onto his porch. "What the hell is all the commotion about?" He looked between the three of us and Phoenix's wolf. "Oh god," he groaned with an eye roll.

"Stay back, Stone!" Dax yelled. "Just go back inside slowly and you'll be safe."

"For fuck's sake, can somebody *please* just tell him?"

"Tell me what?" Dax asked, looking back at me. While he was distracted, Rory slipped away from behind him and approached his mate. "Rory, no!" Dax yelled when he looked forward again.

"It's okay," I assured Dax, rubbing my hands up and down his arms. "I promise you that wolf would never hurt Rory."

"What is he, some kind of pet or something?"

Stone laughed out loud from his porch. "Yes! *Exactly* like a pet!" Phoenix growled out his frustration at Stone's enjoyment.

"Don't you dare growl at my friend!" Dax shouted. He quickly removed his sneaker and threw it, hitting Phoenix square in the nose. Stone doubled over with laughter. "I've got another one where that came from!" Dax threatened, removing his other shoe.

"Do it!" Stone howled.

"Baby, if you don't want to get hit with more shoes, I think you better shift so that Dax can see who you are," Rory told his mate, who tucked his ears back and lowered his head. "Are you not wanting to shift because you're naked?" Phoenix nodded.

"Holy shit, it's like he can understand him," Dax whispered, and Stone went into another laughing fit.

"Stop! Please, I'm gonna piss myself!"

"I'll shield you," Rory promised his mate. "Dax needs to learn about this stuff anyway, and this will be the quickest way. I won't let him see any of your goodies, okay? Just shift."

Snaps and cracks filled the air as Phoenix's body contorted and transitioned. After just a few seconds, a human Phoenix stood before us, with Rory shielding his 'goodies' just like he promised.

"See?" Rory asked Dax with a smile. "It's okay; it's just Phoenix."

"It's just Phoenix," Dax repeated in a faraway voice. "Just...wolf...man..." He tumbled backwards and I caught him in my arms.

"Dax? Dax, are you okay?" I asked him, but it was no good. He was out cold. I scooped him into my arms bridal style as Rory jogged over to us.

"Shit, I wasn't expecting that."

"He's just so overwhelmed by everything that's happened today," I said as

I gently brushed my fingers over his bruise. "My poor, sweet mate."

"What happened to him?" Stone asked as he and Phoenix approached. Our Alpha was no longer concerned with his nudity since we'd all seen him countless times.

"His piece of shit ex-boyfriend hit him," Rory spat.

"Oh, fuck no," Stone growled. *Three for three.* "Nobody messes with one of ours." Stone was gruff, but also fiercely loyal. He'd defend his friends until his dying breath. "How should we play this?"

"I say we kill Justin and make it look like an accident," I snarled.

Stone's face nearly split with a blinding grin. "Where has *this* Rowan been? I like your style."

"But we can't," I sighed. "As much as I'd love to string Justin up by the balls, I don't think more violence is the answer. We all just need to be here for Dax."

"I agree," Rory nodded. "You saw how upset he got when we were talking about you and Phoenix shoving Justin's head up his own ass."

Stone's jaw dropped. "*What*? You left me out of all the fun?"

"Of course not," Rory assured. "Two people need to hold his ass open while the third one does the shoving."

"Good idea," Stone nodded. "You guys are impressing the hell out of me today."

"We'll keep that plan on the back burner," I promised to appease Stone. "Right now, I need to get my mate inside and comfortable."

"I've got his shoes," Phoenix said, and Stone gave another little chuckle.

I carried Dax to my home and into my bedroom. "Guys, can I ask for a favor?" All three of my friends nodded and my chest warmed. "Can you please change my sheets? I wallowed in these for four days, and I want my mate to be comfortable."

"Of course," Rory smiled before stripping the bed and carrying the sheets toward the laundry. Phoenix and Stone worked together to quickly re-dress the mattress. Once everything was set, I placed Dax gently in the center of the bed, cradling his head against my softest pillow.

"Is there anything else you need?" Phoenix asked after Dax was settled.

"I can't think of anything."

"Well, let us know if you do. And congratulations; I knew he'd come back."

"Thank you, Alpha." Phoenix smiled and squeezed my shoulder.

"He's a fighter," Stone said proudly as he looked over my unconscious mate. "I like him."

"Thanks, Stone. And thank you both for everything the past few days."

"Think nothing of it," Phoenix said with a wave of his hand while Stone nodded his agreement.

"Hey Rowan?" When I looked at Rory, he was chewing on his lip. "I know this probably isn't what you want to hear, but...when Dax wakes up, I think it might be a good idea for me to be here with him...alone. It's just that he's been through some shit today and he'll need me. Not that he won't need you or want you too," he said quickly, holding up his hands. "I just think...well…"

"It's okay, Rory." I stepped toe to toe with him and placed my hands on his shoulders. "I know you two are very close, and I'm sure he will want to speak with you when he wakes up. I'm happy to give you two some time alone, but please call for me if he needs anything, okay?"

"I will." Rory gave me a sweet smile. "I'm thankful you're his mate."

I pulled him into a swift hug. "I'm thankful you're his friend."

Rory took a seat on the side of the mattress and took Dax's hand. After Phoenix

gave his mate a kiss, he, Stone and I left
Rory and Dax alone. There was something I
wanted to do before my mate woke up.

Chapter Five

Dax

I groaned as the pain in my face and head hit me as I started to wake up.

"Shh, it's okay," a quiet voice comforted. "I'm here." Someone was sitting close to me and holding my hand.

"Rowan?" I asked hopefully, and received a little chuckle.

"No, it's me."

I peeled my eyes open and blinked away their sensitivity to the light. "Rory?" My friend smiled at me, and I looked all around the room to see that we were alone. "Where's Rowan?"

"Tsk tsk," Rory teased with a shake of his head. "You get a hot new piece of ass in your life and forget all about your best friend."

"I'm sorry. Of course I'm glad to see you."

"I'm only playing," he insisted with a squeeze of my hand. "Rowan will be back soon. You're in his room." *That explains why I smell him.* Rowan always smelled like sandalwood, and it was delicious. I looked around at the simply decorated room with a navy blue comforter on the bed that matched the drapes over the windows. "He brought you here to rest, and I thought you might want to talk when you woke up."

Talk about what? And why was I sleeping? I thought back and everything hit me at once; leaving Justin, talking to Rowan and Rory, and then...the wolf. The wolf that became Phoenix. I must have passed out from shock. I sat up and gave my friend my full attention.

"So...that actually happened? It wasn't some fucked up dream?"

"It was real."

I rubbed at my temples, but flinched when I brushed against the bruise on my face. "But *how*? I know what I saw, but it doesn't make any sense. How does a person turn into an animal? I just...I don't understand."

Rory gave me a little smile and took my hand again. "I've wanted to tell you for a while, but it wasn't something I wanted to talk about over the phone. I figured you'd think I was teasing you; I wanted you to see it for yourself." I definitely wouldn't have believed that shit if I hadn't seen it with my own eyes. Rory tapped his chin. "Now, where to start, where to start…"

He took a deep breath. "Okay, so humans aren't the only beings on earth. There are also shifters, who are people who can transform into animals and back whenever they feel like it. Most people have never heard of them because back in the day, mankind tried to wipe them out because they were afraid of them, so shifters try to keep their identities secret from people to keep themselves safe. Make sense so far?"

I nodded my head slowly. I understood what he was saying even if I didn't understand how it was possible. "Great," he smiled, "Because now we're getting into the weird part."

"Oh, *now* we're getting into the weird shit?" I asked with wide eyes, and Rory just laughed.

"Shifters are also immortal. They are immune to all diseases and stop visual signs of aging after around the age of thirty to forty. They can't get sick and they heal almost immediately if they get hurt because they have super high metabolisms and regeneration. The only way they can die is if you like, stab them in the heart or cut off their head or something."

"Jesus, Roar," I exclaimed, rubbing my head again. I wondered if this was how Phoenix told him everything.

"Sorry. My point is that they're really tough."

"Got it."

"Now brace yourself for the next part."

"How many times do I have to warn you about my cholesterol and being a ticking time bomb?"

Rory blinked at me. "That's why I said brace yourself."

"Right." I took a cleansing breath. "Continue."

"Phoenix is a very special shifter called an Alpha. He was born to lead and protect his own family of shifters, called his pack. Rowan, Stone and I are his pack."

"You're saying...Rowan and Stone are shifters too?" Rory nodded. "And...and you?"

"I'm just a human like always. It's not like the werewolf movies where people turn; you have to be *born* a shifter."

"So how are you in their pack?"

"I'm in the pack because I'm the Alpha's mate. And I'm telling you all about mates next, so you don't have to ask." I smirked at my friend; he knew me so well. "Every shifter has a mate who is fated to them; in other words, Fate picks out who will be perfect for them in every way. Shifters love their mates with their whole heart and will do anything to make them happy. They recognize their person by scent and instinct. Phoenix told me when he smelled and saw me for the first time, his soul automatically knew mine belonged with his; that we needed each other to survive. So, since I'm the Alpha's mate, I automatically became part of the pack and help lead and guide them."

"So you're like the First Lady of the wolves?"

Rory snorted. "Damn straight. Oh, and look at this." He raised his shirt to reveal a tribal-looking wolf tattoo on his chest.

"Holy shit, you got a *tattoo*? But you hate needles! You passed out last year when you got a flu shot!"

"It's not technically a tattoo. Well, I guess it is because it's permanent, but there weren't any needles involved. When Phoenix and I mated, the design appeared on my skin. The whole pack has one."

"So you got a magic tattoo because your boyfriend fucked you?"

Rory laughed and shook his head. "There's a little more to mating than that. To claim their mate, a shifter has to spill their seed inside them and bite a mark into their neck. See?" He pulled his collar to the side to show me a pink scar.

"Oh, excuse me; you got a magic tattoo because your boyfriend fucked you *and* bit you."

He laughed again. "Exactly. But mating isn't just about the sex; Phoenix and I are joined spiritually and physically. He hurts when we're apart for more than a couple of hours. Our lifelines are linked together; if he dies, I die, and if I die, he dies. We can't survive without each other. But unless I'm killed, I'm immortal now too. I won't ever get sick. I heal really fast if I get hurt, and I have to eat a ton of food to keep my energy and strength up."

"That all sounds so incredible."

"But the *best* part is that ever since the moment Phoenix saw me, he can never love or desire anyone else. Things will never cool down between us, and we'll only fall deeper in love. When we mated, it bound our souls together. It's like a marriage on steroids. I even call him my wolf husband."

"Wolf husband," I snickered. "That's cute. I'm just glad there wasn't an *actual* wedding because I'd have to throw a royal hissy fit over not being your best man."

"I'd never have a wolf wedding without you," he promised and I laughed again. "Seriously though, it's been killing me keeping all of this from you."

"I understand why you needed to, but thank you for explaining it all to me." It would have raised some serious red flags when my ass was growing old and crusty and Rory still looked fresh. "It's crazy but wonderful and I'm so happy for you, Roar. You deserve all of this and more." He squeezed my hand and gave me a loving smile. "So, Stone and Rowan have mates out there somewhere too?" The thought of Rowan being mated to someone hurt a thousand times worse than Justin punching my face, but I had to know.

"Stone isn't exactly hurting himself looking for his mate. Don't get me wrong; all shifters want their mate and when Stone meets his, he'll love him fully and endlessly, but he's okay with a little wait. Rowan...well, Rowan..." Rory tucked his bottom lip between his teeth. "He um..."

There was a gentle knock on the door and Rowan's voice called, "May I come in?"

"Right on time," Rory sighed. *What the hell does that mean?*

I forgot my question when Rowan entered the room and gave me a heart stopping smile. "Hey, cookie." The pet name sent me melting right into the mattress. "How are you feeling?"

Better now that your fine ass is here. "I'm okay."

"I have something for you." He brought his arm around from behind his back, revealing a mason jar full of wildflowers in his hand.

"They're beautiful," I whispered. "Thank you."

"You're welcome." He placed the jar on the nightstand beside me. "I also made this for you." In his other hand, he held a small ceramic pot. "It will help take the pain and swelling out of your face, and help the bruise heal quickly; it's a cream blended with arnica and witch hazel."

"No wonder plant cinnamon?" I teased, and Rowan beamed.

"Okay, well, I think you're in good hands," Rory said as he stood from the bed. I felt a little bad; I'd forgotten he was even in the room. "Get some rest and I'll see you in the morning, okay?" He leaned in to give me a hug. "Love you."

"Love you too."

Rory stopped on his way out of the room to give Rowan a hug as well.

"Thank you," Rowan whispered to my friend, and Rory gave him a wink in return.

"Tell the wolf husband I said hello," I added before Rory left the room with a chuckle. I turned my attention to Rowan as he sat on the side of the bed, facing me. "So...you're a shifter. That's...wow." I wasn't sure what to say.

"Does it frighten you?"

"No." That I *was* sure of. "I'll admit it was a shock to see Phoenix changing from wolf to man, but once Rory explained everything to me, it's actually really cool. And he seems insanely happy."

"Rory has been a blessing to our pack. He's kind and loyal and has made our Alpha 'insanely happy'." He winked and lifted the small pot in his hand. "May I put some of this on you?" I nodded and he scooped a blob of lotion onto his fingers. Rowan gently pressed his fingertips to my cheek and rubbed the cream in small circles. "Does that feel okay?"

"It feels great." The lotion was cool and took the sting out of my skin.

Rowan finished rubbing it in and placed the pot on the nightstand next to my flowers. I loved the little bundle of yellow and purple blossoms; it was the first bouquet I'd ever received.

"That will get you feeling better really soon." He thumbed over my bruise again and gave me a sad smile. "I'm just so sorry this happened to you. I'll never forgive myself for not being there to protect you."

His words both surprised me and warmed my heart. "Rowan, none of this is your fault. Like you said; the only person who's in the wrong here is Justin. I tried to keep him happy; I cooked and cleaned and worked my ass off to take care of him and to try and save our relationship. But none of it mattered because he didn't *want* a relationship. He wanted a maid, a chef, and a paycheck. It took me too long to realize that I deserve better."

"You deserve the world," Rowan replied seriously. "You deserve a man who will appreciate your kind heart and beautiful soul; a man who will treat you like the treasure you are."

"Thank you," I whispered. Everything he said to me was exactly what I'd always longed to hear. His words gave me peace and hope; not to mention a wicked case of butterflies in my gut. Being near him made me happy and...whole. "Before I got distracted by Phoenix in wolf form, I was going to tell you something," I reminded him, and Rowan nodded for me to continue. "But...now I'm not sure I should."

He tipped his head to the side. "Why not?"

"Well, Rory told me all about shifters and their mates. He told me that you have a mate too somewhere, and that you two are fated to be together."

A tender smile crossed Rowan's lips. "It's true."

My heart dropped. As much as I wanted to be with Rowan, I couldn't do it. I couldn't tell him how I felt about him; even if he felt the same way, which I thought maybe he did, I'd always be the placeholder. I'd be his boyfriend until he met his fated mate, and then I'd be replaced and it would break my heart.

"He'll be a very lucky man when he meets you," I told him honestly. I couldn't imagine a better mate than Rowan; he was protective, thoughtful, sweet, and easy to talk to.

"I've already met him, and I can assure you I'm the lucky one," Rowan countered, and his words were like a punch to the balls. I felt nauseous and my eyes prickled with emotion. "He's absolutely perfect. He's funny and-"

"Please," I interrupted him in a shaky voice. "I know it's stupid and I'm embarrassing myself, but I...I can't hear about you with someone else." I rubbed the intense pain that bloomed in my chest at the words. "It hurts too bad."

"Oh, sweet Dax, I don't think you understand." Rowan placed a hand to my cheek and gave me a soft smile. "*You* are my perfect mate."

My chest heaved as I tried to catch my breath, which had left me in a rush. "I am? So everything Rory said about mating and eternal life and healing..."

I lost my train of thought, but Rowan seemed to understand anyway as he nodded. "I knew you before I even met you. I caught your scent on Rory and Phoenix after your visit with them a couple of weeks ago, and then again when you came to us several days ago."

"What do I smell like?"

"Like vanilla." A smile slowly crossed his lips and he added, "And cinnamon."

"Super plant," I whispered and Rowan gave a little chuckle. "But I don't understand; if you knew I was your mate, why didn't you tell me?" Realization hit me and my heart dropped again. "Were you disappointed? Because I know I'm not the best looking guy, but like I said, I can cook and clean and-"

"Shh, shh," Rowan quieted me, taking both of my hands. "Dax, I could *never* be disappointed with you. I meant it when I said you were the most beautiful man I'd ever seen. I will only ever desire your body; no one else's, because yours is perfect for me. *You* are perfect for me. The only reason I didn't tell you is because I overheard you talking to Rory that night. You were upset about having feelings for me and wanted to try working things out with Justin. Even though I wanted you with every fiber of my being, I would never force you to accept me. I wanted your happiness, even if it wasn't with me."

"And I must apologize for your illness," he continued. "It was because we were apart. Your body and soul were mourning not having me close to you. I hoped that if you were truly happy with Justin, it would negate the effects of the mate pull."

"Were you sick too?"

Rowan nodded and rubbed his thumbs over the backs of my hands. "I couldn't leave my bed and Rory had to feed me. Being away from you was misery."

"I'm so sorry."

"Don't be." He lifted my right hand and kissed my knuckles. "We are together now and that's all that matters. And as far as you saying you can cook and clean...Dax, I can do those things too. I don't want a maid or a chef or a paycheck. I want a lover;

someone I can dote on, protect, and cherish. Someone to share my eternal life with."

"As equals?"

"No, Dax. We will never be equals." It hurt to hear, but I supposed it made sense; he was a strong, powerful shifter and I was just a human. "You are my king and I promise to always treat you as such; to put you on a pedestal and do everything I can to one day deserve you."

In a flash, I gripped the collar of his sweater in both hands and pulled him down to me, crashing our lips together. Rowan tensed for a moment before melting against me. He snaked one arm around my waist and cupped his other hand on the back of my neck. His touch was gentle; he held me tenderly and carefully, like a precious treasure.

And the kiss? Holy hell, the kiss. It was sweet and chaste, and yet the hottest thing I'd ever experienced. Rowan hummed as he pecked my lips with his, which were soft and plush. He nipped and nibbled every centimeter of my skin from my moustache to my scruffy chin before pulling back and sighing happily.

"Thank you, Dax," he whispered before slowly opening his eyes. His pupils were wide and shimmering with adoration. "My first kiss was even more wonderful than I imagined it would be."

I narrowed my eyes. "You mean your first kiss with your mate?" He shook his head no and my heart nearly exploded.

"I waited my whole life for you. I didn't want to experience anything with a man who wasn't my mate. I wanted all of my firsts to be with you."

Holy. Shit. "Are you upset that *I* didn't wait?" My first kiss was with Justin, although it paled in comparison to what I just shared with Rowan. I also gave my virginity to my ex. The thought now made my stomach turn, but there was nothing I could do about it. I just hoped Rowan didn't hold it against me.

"Of course not. Waiting was *my* choice, but I'd never expect you to do the same. You didn't know anything about me or mates; even if you did, it doesn't make anything between us any less special." He smiled and ran his fingers through my hair. "I love you, Dax." I gasped and he added quickly, "Please don't feel like you have to say it back. I know things are different for humans. I just wanted to tell you how I feel about you."

"I feel the same way about you," I replied, and Rowan's eyes widened. "The thing is, because of my time with Justin, I know what love *isn't*. But my time with you, even though it hasn't been very long, has shown me what it *is*. You treat me with value and respect and I can't thank you enough for that. I love you, Rowan. I've known practically since the moment I met you. I was scared and guilty, but couldn't deny it. That's what I came back to tell you."

Rowan's gaze flicked quickly between my eyes. "I'm so happy I'm not sure what to do."

A saucy smile took over my lips. "I can think of one thing."

I pulled him into another kiss, and he quickly wrapped his arms around me again. This time, I trailed my hands from the collar of his sweater up his neck and into his soft hair. It was just long enough to twist around my fingers and felt like silk against my skin.

I stuck out the tip of my tongue and ran it slowly across the seam of Rowan's lips, and his jaws sprang open. I slipped my tongue into his mouth and licked against his as he shuddered and moaned. It only took a moment for him to taste me back; at first, it was a gentle lapping against my tongue and cheeks, but soon, we were locked in a desperate, passionate frenzy.

Our tongues curled around each other, blending our flavors into an intense sweet taste that danced across my tongue and made my brain fuzzy. Rowan pulled me as close to him as possible and I tightened my fingers in his hair until he moaned into my mouth.

In a blink, Rowan tightened his hold around my waist, laid back onto the mattress and pulled me on top of him. I flinched and ripped my lips from his.

"I'm sorry, is this too much?" he asked worriedly.

"No, this is amazing. It's just...I'm not hurting you, am I?"

He gave me an understanding smile. "No, cookie. I love the warmth and pressure of your body on top of mine. It's the most incredible thing I've ever felt."

I attacked his lips like a wild man. I kissed, nipped and tasted until we were both breathless. But it wasn't enough. His touch lit a fire in me and I needed more. I wanted to feel him; to taste him. I wanted to show my appreciation for his body as he'd done for mine. I wanted him to feel my love.

I peeled my lips from his. "Row, can I give you another first?" He nodded enthusiastically and I chuckled. "Don't you want to know what it is?"

"I'm yours, Dax. Do whatever you wish to me and I know it will be magical."

Well damn. I was clueless as to how everything that came out of his mouth made me weak in the knees, but too turned on to give it much thought. I propped up so that I was straddling him and inched his sweater up his abdomen. My jaw dropped when I got my first glimpse of his body. My hands stilled from shock and Rowan took over, pulling his shirt the rest of the way off and tossing it to the floor.

His abdomen and chest were smooth and sculpted. Deep creases ran between mounds of muscle. There was no fluff under his skin; everything was tight and firm. My eyes tracked to the pretty tribal wolf that was printed on his left pec. My heart beat wildly at the thought that I'd have one someday too; not from fear, but excitement. But today wasn't the day. Today I just wanted to do something special for Rowan; to give him something special he'd never experienced before.

"Your body is gorgeous," I whispered as I went back to exploring his form with my eyes. I couldn't believe I was with someone so sexy.

"Thank you. May I see yours as well?" he asked, curling his fingers around the hem of my t-shirt but making no further movement without my permission.

Doubt and insecurity instantly clouded my mind. I didn't look anything like Rowan. I was all fluff and no firm. I didn't want to disappoint him. I took a deep breath to settle my nerves. *He said you could never disappoint him. He's not like Justin. He loves you, Dax. You're his mate.* I nodded and Rowan beamed.

He quickly removed my shirt and his smile disappeared as his eyes tracked over my body. "Wow." *Is that a good wow or a bad wow?* He pressed both of his palms to my soft belly that rounded out over the button of my jeans. He gently caressed over my abdomen and up my soft chest, both of which were covered in fine reddish-brown hair. He didn't stop until his hands cupped my furry cheeks. "Your beauty takes my breath away."

I sighed in relief. His smile disappeared in reverence, not from dissatisfaction. I leaned over to kiss him again, but stopped when he gasped quietly. "Your skin is so soft and warm against mine," he explained quietly.

I pecked his lips again before trailing mine down the side of his neck. Rowan moaned quietly and I smiled against his skin; I hadn't even gotten to the good parts yet. I kissed across his collarbone and down his pec. When I flicked my tongue across his nipple, Rowan nearly flew off of the mattress.

I huffed a laugh and continued on my path down his abdomen. I slid my tongue into the deep grooves in his skin and gently nipped his slabs of muscle.

"Oh Dax, this feels so incredible."

I looked up to find he had his head propped up with his hands so that he could watch me. "Row, you haven't felt anything yet," I told him with a wink. His eyes widened when I popped the button of his jeans. I'd never been so bold in bed, but knowing Rowan felt so strongly for me and enjoyed what I was doing gave me courage.

I unzipped his pants and worked the denim down his legs. I pulled off his boots and socks and tossed them and his jeans onto the floor. I swallowed hard at the sight of the long, thick lump in his boxer briefs. I peeled down the fabric and my eyes nearly popped out of my skull. I don't remember fully removing his underwear, but suddenly he was before me in all of his glory. And sweet veiny meat, was he glorious. His dick was nearly eight inches long, thick, and uncut. His balls hung heavy and were covered in coarse dark brown hair.

I touched the tip of my tongue to Rowan's slit and a shudder quaked through his body. He groaned, "Ohhh god," and I smiled again. It was so special to be giving these things to him and witnessing his first ever reactions. I flattened my tongue against his tip and rotated my head in slow circles as he groaned again, long and low. The salty tang of his pre-cum coated my tongue and spurred me on.

I closed my mouth around his crown and sucked as I slid my lips down his length. I wasn't able to take him fully into my throat, but Rowan didn't seem to mind. He whimpered and moaned as I bobbed my head up and down, swallowing up his cock.

"Oh Dax," he chanted over and over as I quickened my pace. I sucked hard, took as much as him down my throat as possible, and bounced my head quickly. I cupped his fuzzy balls in my palm and squeezed them gently as Rowan cried out his pleasure. "Dax, I, please, yes, oh god…" He wasn't making any sense and I loved it. It meant I was giving him the brain-scrambling experience I hoped for.

I wrapped my free hand around the base of his cock and pumped my wrist in time with my lips, covering every delicious inch of him. My arm cramped up and my face stung, but I pushed through it. I only stroked him faster and sucked harder.

Rowan screamed my name and I wasn't sure if it was rapture or warning, as his cock throbbed in my mouth and dumped salty seed onto my tongue. I swallowed rapidly, greedily taking every warm mouthful into my own body. I licked slow circles around his tip until Rowan was trembling and making the sweetest whimpering sounds.

He didn't move when I crawled up beside him and lay my head on his chest, which was still heaving for breath. His eyes were closed and his brow was pinched in.

"Are you okay?" I whispered. He blinked his eyes open and looked at me. A goofy smile stretched across his lips.

"I'm wonderful." He cupped my cheek in a shaky hand. "Thank you, my love. That was incredible. May I try for you?"

I blinked in surprise. "Seriously?"

"Unless you don't want me to, of course. I would never push you. I only want to show you how special you are to me and make you feel good."

"No, no, I want you to." I'd be an idiot not to want his perfect, pouty lips on me. "I was just surprised, that's all. No one's ever done that for me. Justin wouldn't dream of it and-" I flinched when a low growl sounded in Rowan's chest.

"I'm sorry. I can't control my anger when it comes to that man." Before I could apologize for bringing him up, Rowan's face softened. "Justin is an arrogant pig who doesn't know how to treat a man. Let me show you a real man's love." I nodded slowly because my tongue was suddenly numb.

Rowan eased me onto my back and hovered above me. He slowly and meticulously kissed every inch of my chest as he scooted backward. When he reached my stomach, he rubbed his cheek against it. "I love the hair on your body; it tickles my skin gently, but makes you look so manly and handsome. You're like a rugged teddy bear." It was the strangest, yet most beautiful compliment I'd ever received because it came straight from his heart.

Once he got his fill of nuzzling my belly, Rowan unbuttoned my jeans. He pulled them and my underwear down and off in one tug, but left my socks on. "I don't want your feet to get cold," he explained, and I was once again stunned by his thoughtfulness.

Rowan kissed up the front of my legs until he was eye level with my dick. I held my breath for his appraisal; I was about six and a half inches long, cut and medium thickness. Not too shabby, but nothing to brag about either. "Oh Dax, you're perfect." He pressed his nose into my trimmed pubes and breathed in my scent deeply, reminding me he was part animal. It was raw and primal and hot as hell.

I cried out when Rowan deepthroated my dick. I wasn't expecting it but I damn sure enjoyed it. Unlike me, he was able to swallow every inch of my cock down his throat. He sucked hard and wasted no time setting a rapid pace. He gobbled me down again and again as his hand cupped around my balls. He squeezed and bounced my flesh in his palm and I was on the edge in no time.

The words, "Row, I'm not gonna last," were barely past my lips when my balls tightened and pulled up toward my body. I grunted as my dick jerked in his mouth and I came hard between his lips. Rowan moaned as he swallowed all I gave him and licked my skin clean. He kept lapping at my spent dick until I saw stars in my vision and I unfortunately had to ask him to stop. It was too good to handle.

He climbed up beside me and pulled me into his arms. I once again rested my head on his firm chest. I listened to his heartbeat as he caressed my back and repeatedly kissed the top of my head.

I ruined our beautiful moment when my stomach growled loudly, filling the room with what sounded like a whale song. "I'm so sorry. I haven't eaten much the past few days and I guess it's catching up with me."

"Don't be sorry, cookie." Rowan stood up from the bed and patted one of the big, fluffy pillows at the top. "Why don't you get comfortable and I'll make us a couple of sandwiches? If you want, we can watch a scary movie together while we eat." He pointed to a TV on the wall past the foot of his bed. "Then I'll snuggle you under the covers and keep you warm all night long."

I swallowed hard, trying to keep my emotions at bay. This wonderful man wanted to meet my needs by making me something to eat, and then was looking forward to sharing a bed with me instead of complaining that I took up too much space. He couldn't be more different from my ex if he tried, and I was so goddamn thankful for him.

Rowan looked concerned as he asked, "Is something wrong?"

"I just love you so fucking much."

Chapter Six

Rowan

"Don't tell me, I know this one," Dax
said as he studied the bush along the path.

After we woke up and I made us a big
breakfast of eggs, bacon and toast, Dax
asked if I would take him on some of the
easy trails through the state forest and teach
him about the flora that grew around them.
Now he was trying to impress me with his
memory. He didn't have to try; though I *was*
impressed by his attentiveness and
willingness to learn, I just enjoyed spending
this time with him.

"It's...buckthorn?" he asked with his
face scrunched up in uncertainty.

"You got it," I smiled and Dax
punched his fist into the air. "I'm so proud of
you."

"I've got a really great teacher," he
smiled back. He stepped up to me and
wrapped his arms around my waist. I

hugged him back and laid my cheek against the top of his head. "Thank you for showing me all of this. I'm having a really good time."

"It's my pleasure. I love being outdoors and there's no one I'd rather share this beautiful day with." Not many trees had leaves remaining, but those that were still hanging on were beautiful shades of orange and red. Though the sun was shining, the autumn air had a nip to it, so we were bundled up in jackets.

"I just still can't believe I'm out hiking," Dax chuckled. "It normally wouldn't be on the top of my to-do list, but you make it fun. I'm sure you'd make *anything* fun, though." I smiled and gave his forehead a kiss. "And I appreciate you sticking to the easy paths with me. I'm afraid I'm not ready for steep hills yet." He backed away from my chest to look up at me. "And you're positive you're not getting bored?"

"I could never be bored when I'm with you," I assured him. "And I like all of the trails. If you decide you want to go on a difficult one, I'll be happy to take you. If you get tired, I'll just carry you the rest of the way."

"I swear, sometimes it's hard to believe you're even real."

I chuckled and shook my head at my silly man. "Would you like for me to show you something else?"

"Of course."

I led him by the hand to a couple of tall trees. "These trees are very common around here. They are white oak and red oak, and there's a very easy way to tell them apart." I knelt to the ground and picked up two different leaves. I stood and held them out for Dax to inspect. One had sharp edges made up of multiple points, while the other had smooth, rounded edges.

"So which one is which?"

"This one is the red oak," I replied, holding up the jagged leaf. "The way I remember it is that its edges look sharp, like they could cut me, and red is the color of blood."

"I'll definitely remember that because it's kind of creepy," Dax smiled. I learned just how much my mate liked creepy things when we watched a scary movie together last night. He chose a movie about a demon possession, including head spinning and disembodied voices. It freaked the hell out of me, but Dax just kept gushing about how 'awesome' it was.

"And this one is white oak," I continued, holding up the smooth leaf. "Its edges are rounded and dull, like an egg."

"Which is white," Dax concluded, his smile widening. "Mm, mm, mm, brains, beauty, *and* brawn. Mr. Triple Threat and you're all mine." He captured me in another hug as I laughed again. He made me so happy I couldn't hold it all in.

I kissed the tip of his nose and flinched when I felt how cold it was against my lips. "Your nose is freezing, cookie. I better get you back inside." He nodded, but he didn't move, and he chewed on his bottom lip like he was nervous about something. "What's wrong?"

Dax looked at his feet and kicked his toe into the dirt path. "Well, I'm wondering something but I'm kind of embarrassed to bring it up. I mean I think I know the answer, but it'll be more embarrassing if I'm wrong."

I blinked in confusion. "Dax, you never need to be embarrassed around me. You can ask me anything. If I don't know the answer, we'll find out together."

He let out a long breath before nodding. "I know you wanted me to stay with you last night and I loved it. And since I'm... you know, your mate, I know you need me close to you." He looked up at me and I nodded, unsure where this was going. "I guess I was just wondering...do you want me to *stay* with you or should I stay with Roar? Or maybe like on Stone's couch or something so I won't bother the newlyweds? I don't want to assume anything and invade your space."

"Oh, Dax." I circled my arms around him and held him tight. "I'm so sorry. I forget that this is all new to you. I want and need you with me. Everything that belongs to me also belongs to you, including our home. Again, it's your choice, but I ask that you please stay with me."

"I'd love to." I squeezed him harder and gave his head another kiss. "I'm just sorry I don't have more to bring to the table; basically all I own is what I brought in my duffel bag."

"You've given me your humor and heart, and that is more than I'll ever need."

"How the hell do you always know what to say?" I chuckled and rubbed my hands in circles across his back. "Hey, since we're out here, will you show me one more thing?"

"Anything."

"Can I see your wolf? Or...you *as* a wolf?" He scrunched up his face. "Am I saying that right?"

"You're saying it perfectly and I'd be happy to show you. Just remember, when I'm in my wolf form, I'm in total control. You don't have to be frightened." Dax nodded and his eyes widened when I unzipped my jacket, so I explained, "I'm removing my clothes so they don't rip when I shift."

"Oh, I like this already." He took a seat on the ground, ready for the show.

I laughed and dropped my coat and sweater to the ground. I kicked off my boots and made quick work of my pants and underwear as Dax hungrily eyeballed my body, whispering '*So damn sexy*' under his breath.

Before I got too distracted by my mate's wanton stare and the smell of his arousal in the air, I began the shifting process. My organs relocated and my bones snapped, reforming into a wolf's skeleton. Hair sprouted from my skin and claws burst from my hands, which were now large paws.

I took a deep breath and smelled my mate's sweet aroma even stronger with my enhanced senses. I stepped toward him to get a bigger sniff, but Dax flinched when I neared. His fists clenched and panic showed in his eyes, so I froze in my tracks.

"I'm sorry," he squeaked out. "It's just that I've never been this close to a dangerous animal." He flinched again. "Not that I think you're dangerous! You're just bigger than I thought you'd be. And you look exactly like a wolf. Shit, that sounds so stupid; of course you look like a wolf. I don't know what I was expecting." He dropped his face in his hands. "Please don't hate me. You hate me, don't you?"

I could never hate my mate, and I understood his reaction, but I couldn't tell him in this form. I didn't want to shift yet; I wanted Dax to grow more comfortable around my wolf and see that I would never harm him. I trotted over to the edge of the path and clamped my teeth around a grape hyacinth, one of the few wildflowers left standing. I ripped it from the dirt and slowly approached my mate again.

I nudged his thigh with my nose and he gasped slightly when he raised his head. When he noticed the flower in my mouth, the fear melted from his face and was replaced with a gentle smile.

"Is that for me?" I nodded and dropped the slightly slobbery flower onto his leg. "Thank you. You're still my big sweetheart, aren't you?" I tucked my ears back and lowered my head in the most non-threatening action I knew. "I'm sorry it took me a minute. You're just so strong. I guess I shouldn't be surprised since you're so strong in human form too." He scrubbed a hand over his beard. "That's the weirdest thing

I've ever said." I chuffed and he narrowed his eyes. "Did you just laugh at me?" I worried I'd offended him, but he just smiled wider. "That's amazing."

Dax slowly raised his hand toward my head. "May I?" I nodded and he tentatively touched the top of my skull. He stroked my head and trailed his hand to the side, scratching behind my ear. He laughed when I let out a throaty moan of pleasure. "You like that?" At my nod, Dax lifted his other hand and gave both of my ears a thorough scratching. "There you go."

I licked the side of his face and he laughed again. It made my heart sing that he was accepting of both of my forms and was no longer afraid. I laid down beside him and placed my head in his lap, and Dax caressed his hands over my head and down my back.

"I think this is my new favorite thing," he whispered, burrowing his fingers into my wiry fur. We stayed that way for a long time;

Dax petting me while the cool breeze rustled my hair and blew a myriad of scents past my sensitive nose, though none were as sweet as my mate's natural aroma.

Though I was happier and more comfortable than ever before, I knew it was time to head back inside when Dax shivered. I was warm beneath my thick coat of fur, but his jacket wasn't enough to fight off the chill in the air.

I stood up and backed a few steps away before letting the transition take over. Bones slid into place, my ears lowered, my snout shortened and I reared up on two legs. Seconds later, I stood in human form before my mate. I offered him my hand and pulled him to his feet as well.

"Does it hurt when you shift?" Dax asked with concern in his eyes, and my heart swelled at his care.

"Not at all. It feels like a big stretch."

"Good." I smiled and picked my jeans up off of the ground. "It's a shame you have to cover up that perfect body with all of those clothes."

"I can walk back home naked if you wish, but everyone will see."

"Let me help you with your shirt." I laughed at his reaction; being nude around my friends didn't bother me, but I loved that Dax was territorial over my body.

"I had an idea for this evening I thought you might enjoy," I told Dax when I was fully dressed again. "I thought I could show you how to build a fire and we could invite our friends to roast hot dogs with us."

"Really? That sounds awesome!" His smile died and he gave me a serious look. "But I have one question before I agree to this."

"What is it?" Whatever he wanted, I'd make it happen.

"Do you have marshmallows?"

I laughed out loud at the sincere way he asked the silly question. I lowered my mouth to his ear and whispered, "A whole bag." Dax gave a full body shudder when I added, "I've got chocolate and graham crackers too."

He took my hand and pulled me along the path. "Then what are we waiting for?"

Chapter Seven

Dax

"Hold up. So you're saying you guys killed eleven men here just a few weeks ago?" I asked, looking around the land surrounding us. Rowan chose a flat portion of the clearing away from the cabins and trees for our fire, and he, Stone, Phoenix and Rory were filling me in on pack history while we sat around it and ate.

"We had to, cookie," Rowan explained gently. "They attacked us and it was kill or be killed."

"I know," I said quickly, taking his hand. I didn't want him to think I was offended in any way. "I'm just impressed. You guys were so outnumbered and you took care of business."

"Oh, I like this guy," Stone replied with a wicked grin.

"And Roar, you kicked some serious ass too," I gushed, looking at my friend. "I had no idea you knew how to fight."

"Stone taught me everything I know."

"Could you teach me too?" I asked the huge man, who smiled wider.

"Hell yeah. I'll give you one of my knives too and show you how to use it. Everyone should know how to protect themselves."

"Thank you," Rowan and I both told him. It warmed my heart that my safety meant so much to my lover.

"Who's ready for dessert?" Phoenix asked, holding up a bag of marshmallows. We all raised our hands. I'd just finished my third hot dog and surprisingly ate the least of the whole group. Phoenix and Stone each took out eight, Rowan ate seven, and even Rory tackled five. He wasn't kidding when he said shifters and their mates needed to eat a lot. I was excited for that part. Not gonna lie; not only being allowed to but *required* to eat all I wanted was kind of a dream come true.

Phoenix passed the bag around the circle and we all stuck a few little white pillows onto our pointed sticks. Stone sharpened them with one of his knives while Rowan helped me build the fire. Stone kept an alarming number of knives on his person at all times. I wouldn't want to get on his bad side; things could get stabby real quick. I was positive Rowan had an aggressive, dangerous side as well, but *also* positive he'd never turn it on me or anyone he cared about.

He was so patient when he helped me build the fire. He explained why this spot was perfect and how to prepare the area. He showed me how to place the kindling and stack the logs in a pyramid shape. My pyramid collapsed three times, but Rowan didn't get frustrated. He just smiled and helped me reposition the wood. When I finally got the fire going after thorough instruction and multiple attempts, he scooped me into his arms and spun me around, gushing about how proud he was of me. I was pretty damn proud of myself too.

"How do you like your marshmallows cooked?" Rowan asked me as he hovered his stick over the fire.

"Lightly toasted; just enough to get the middle all melty so that it squishes out between the graham crackers."

"Me too," he smiled.

"None of you know what's good," Stone grumbled, shoving his marshmallow deep into the flames.

I wrinkled up my nose. "Are you one of those people who like their marshmallows black and crispy?"

"You mean the correct way? Yes."

"How is that the correct way?" Rory questioned.

Stone let out an exasperated huff. "The way you all cook them, you only get one marshmallow. I get the outside all crispy, peel it off, and eat it. Then I start again on the next layer. I get like *five* marshmallows this way."

"Yeah, five nasty, charcoal-flavored marshmallows," I argued. "Who the hell wants that?"

"Me," Stone shrugged before blowing the flaming treat on the end of his stick. Once it was extinguished, he peeled off the crispy, blackened skin and ate it as I shuddered in disgust.

"I've got your graham crackers and chocolate prepared when you're ready for them," Rowan offered, holding the sandwich out towards me.

"Aw, thank you." I leaned in and pressed my lips to his.

"For the love," Stone groaned around a mouthful of charcoal. "You guys are as disgusting as these two." He thumbed over to Rory and Phoenix, who were kissing deeply.

"You'll be just as disgusting when you find *your* mate," I pointed out, but Stone just rolled his eyes.

"I'll love the shit out of him, but I can't picture myself giving him a mushy nickname or constantly kissing him."

"Wanna bet?" I asked, and he raised his eyebrow. "Ten bucks says you'll be just as gross with your own mate." Sure, he was gruff, but I knew he had a soft side in there too.

"Okay," he nodded. "It's a bet."

"I want in on that action," Rory said, peeling his lips from Phoenix's. "I think he'll be even grosser."

"I'm not sure," Phoenix argued. "I've known Stone for a long time; he's a stubborn son of a bitch. He may reel his emotions back just to prove you two wrong."

"Thank you," Stone replied with a bow of his head. *Wait, was that a compliment?*

"So," Phoenix continued, "My ten dollars says even when he meets his mate,

Stone will be...well, Stone." The big man beamed proudly at the Alpha's words. "What do you say, Rowan?"

"I would never bet against my mate," he answered. "Besides, I now know first hand how powerful the love between mates is. There's no way he can resist a little mushiness."

"Aw, that's so sweet," I told him, and leaned in for another kiss.

"That's it!" Stone barked, standing up. "I'm about to either heave up my hot dogs or jab myself in the eye with this pointy stick. I'm heading home. Goodnight, guys."

"Goodnight," we all answered with a laugh. He stomped off to his cabin and I couldn't help but wonder how much of his feelings were actually disgust and how much were masked jealousy or longing.

Rory climbed into Phoenix's lap and his man cuddled him close. I would've loved to sit on Rowan's lap; I didn't doubt his strength or willingness to hold me, but I *did* question the integrity of the plastic chair he sat in. So instead, I scooted my chair as close as possible to his and laid my head on his shoulder. He wrapped an arm around me and peppered my head with kisses.

The four of us talked for hours until the fire burned down to embers and the air grew colder around us. Our friends excused themselves and Phoenix carried Rory back to their cabin. Rowan showed me how to toss dirt onto the logs to make sure the area was safe to leave unattended.

"Thank you for doing this with me, Row. I had a lot of fun."

"Me too. I enjoy getting together with everyone."

"This won't count as our turn hosting the pack dinner will it?" The others told me about getting together for dinner a few times a week, and I couldn't wait to be a part of it. "Because I'd really like to cook for everyone." I loved cooking, I just didn't like being forced to do it.

"We can still host if you like," Rowan replied with a smile. "It makes me so happy that you enjoy spending time with everyone. I'm looking forward to tasting your cooking since you're excited about it, but remember, I'm always happy to help."

"I know." I gave him a loving grin and took both of his hands in mine. "I know you don't expect me to do anything for you, and I can't tell you how much I appreciate that. You treat me with respect and only have my best interest at heart. You truly love me and I feel the same for you."

"Thank you, cookie." Rowan gave me a gentle kiss and I took a deep breath.

"That's why I want to complete our bond."

Rowan swallowed hard and his eyes darkened. "Are you sure?"

He'd never push me into anything, which only made me want it more. "I've never been more sure of anything. I want you and I want forever *with* you."

"Dax…" His eyes grew misty as he looked into mine. "You've made me happier than I ever dreamed I could be. I promise to spend eternity honoring you and loving you."

"I promise you the same thing." His lips tipped up into the sweetest smile I'd ever seen. "Make me yours, Rowan."

Chapter Eight

Rowan

Dax's eyes widened as I scooped him into my arms and carried him towards our cabin. My heart pounded in my chest with anticipation to claim this wonderful man; to spend forever learning about and laughing with him.

I entered our home, kicked the door shut behind us and didn't stop walking until I stepped inside our bedroom. I laid him gently on our bed and stepped back to admire him. His eyes were brimming with need and his chest rose and fell quickly; he was as eager as I was.

I kicked my boots off under the bed as I untied his and slipped them from his feet. I took his socks off this time; I needed to see every inch of his gorgeous body. Plus, I'd make sure to keep him warm. I unfastened his jeans and pulled them and his underwear down his legs. His hard dick slapped against his belly with a quiet *thud,* and his answering moan spurred me on.

I quickly unzipped his jacket and worked it off of his arms before tossing it to the floor. Dax lifted his arms over his head and allowed me to remove his shirt without struggle. Finally he was bare to me and I wasted no time in soaking up every detail of his soft, luscious body.

"You are so beautiful," I whispered as I caressed my hand down his hairy chest. It was something I doubted he heard often during his last relationship, but what he deserved without question.

"Thank you," he replied just as quietly. "I want to see you too."

I stripped quickly, throwing my clothing in every direction. Soon I was naked, and harder than I'd ever been in my life. My blood surged south, filling my cock until I was firm as stone. My body was desperate to make love to my mate and claim him for all time.

I peeled my eyes from the lovely sight before me to retrieve a bottle of lubricant from my dresser drawer. I'd only used it for 'self love' to handle my biological needs while saving myself for my fated love. I tossed the bottle onto the bed and climbed onto the mattress.

I lowered my body so my skin pressed against his, but kept my weight on my elbows. I took his lips in a long, tender kiss, sweeping the inside of his mouth with my tongue, relishing the sweet flavor of marshmallow and chocolate. Dax hummed against my lips and threaded his fingers into my hair. Our tongues licked and lapped, twisted and tasted until we were breathless.

"I want to make you feel so good," I whispered against his lips.

"Please, Row. I need you."

I kissed down his neck to where it met his shoulder, right where I would place my mark. I sucked a purple love bite onto his skin as Dax moaned and shuddered beneath me.

I continued my trail downward, placing gentle kisses to his chest and stomach as I crawled backward along his body. Dax spread his legs and I sat up on my knees between them. I raised each of his legs and bent them gently, placing the soles of his feet on the bed, opening him up to me. I cupped his plentiful cheeks and squeezed them, moaning aloud when I saw his pucker for the first time.

I pressed my fingertip to his wrinkled flesh. "I can't wait to be inside you."

"God, I need it. Stretch me open, Row; you're so big."

I gripped the lube bottle in my shaking hand and popped open the cap. "I'll take care of you," I promised as I coated my fingers. "I never want to hurt you." I closed the cap and placed the bottle beside my knee.

I touched him again, circling my slick finger over each rise and divot of his flesh. As I massaged, his muscles relaxed beneath my touch. I slid the tip of my finger inside him and Dax let his knees fall apart. I pressed in slowly, sinking my digit into the tight heat of his perfect ass.

"You feel incredible," I told him as I pulsed my finger back and forth. His channel sucked against me and was unlike anything I'd ever experienced.

"Just wait until your thick cock is in there." My hand stuttered to a stop and my eyes widened at his naughty words. "Don't stop," he pleaded, "Give me more."

I slid in a second finger as Dax cursed into the quiet room. I slowly thrust into him, but it wasn't enough for my eager lover. He pushed down against me, burying my fingers inside him. I watched in awe as Dax rode my hand until he was panting.

"More!"

Don't jizz the bed, Rowan. Don't you do it! Dax was so sexy, I feared I'd do exactly that. However, my arousal dampened a bit when Dax hissed with discomfort when I pressed in a third finger. "Are you okay?" I asked quickly.

"I'm good. It just burns a little. Don't stop, though; I need opened up so I can take you."

I nodded my understanding and slowly rocked my hand back and forth. Before long, he loosened up around me and my fingers moved easily within him. I spread them out and circled them around to make sure Dax was prepared.

"I'm ready," he insisted once he was moaning with pleasure again. "Make love to me."

I eased my fingers out of him and grabbed the lube bottle again. I poured so much onto my cock that the liquid slid down onto my balls and dripped onto the blankets beneath me.

I cupped the backs of Dax's knees and pressed them up towards his chest. I touched my soaked tip to his spread opening and looked to him for permission.

"Just go slow, okay?"

"Of course." Not only did I not want to hurt him, I wanted to savor this moment.

Dax took a deep breath and I eased my hips forward. His little hole stretched around my tip, inviting me in. I pushed more firmly and popped through his ring as he hissed again. I remained perfectly still until he nodded for me to continue. I inched forward, sinking inside him as slowly as possible until I was fully submerged in his warm passage.

My eyes rolled back in my head from pleasure; being inside my mate was the greatest, most intense thing I'd ever felt. It took all of my restraint to keep my hips still while Dax adjusted to the intrusion. I forced my eyes open to find his were screwed shut and his cheeks puffed with deep breaths.

"Okay," he panted. "Please move."

Slowly and carefully, I thrust in and out of my lover. Wanting to distract him from any pain, I wrapped my hand around his stiff, leaking cock. I squeezed his flesh gently and stroked his length. It didn't take long for his face to relax into a look of bliss and his measured breaths to morph into whimpers. His muscles loosened and I moved easier within him.

"So good," Dax moaned when I quickened my pace. I rolled my hips, groaning each time I sank into his tight little hole. I pressed his knees closer to his stomach and thrust again, and Dax cried out. "Yes! Oh god, Row, right there! More!"

I snapped my hips back and forth, gliding along the top of his channel to massage his sweet spot. Dax's passage devoured every inch of my cock and squeezed me perfectly. My balls tightened and rolled, but I wanted my mate to get release first.

I bit the inside of my cheek and pumped my wrist faster. I thrust into my lover wildly as he cursed and his back slowly arched off the mattress. His dick swelled in my hand as Dax yelled, "I'm coming!"

Thick white gobs burst from his dick and pooled on his hairy belly. I breathed in the scent deeply and his pheromones threw me over the edge. I cried out my mate's name and buried my cock inside him. My balls climbed and my dick pulsed, releasing a powerful stream of my seed, marking him as mine deep inside.

I eased my cock from his body and rested his legs against the bed. Our stomachs pressed together as I leaned over him. He shuddered when I trailed my fingers over the hickey I left on his neck; I craved to replace it with my bite. I looked at Dax in question and he eagerly nodded.

He gasped when my fangs elongated, so I winked at him, showing he had nothing to fear. He nodded again and I lowered my head to his supple throat. I bit into his flesh, pressing down until my teeth scraped against his collar bone. Dax jerked hard beneath me and another warm burst of his cum splashed between us.

I released my teeth and watched with a smile as his skin knitted into a pretty pink scar, marking him as mine.

"We are eternally bonded," I told him in a reverent whisper. "Our lifelines, bodies and souls are intertwined for all time." A sweet smile crossed his lips and his eyes filled with moisture, which I gently dabbed away. "I love you, Dax. Always."

"I love you too." I kissed him slowly and deeply, pouring my love and adoration into him.

Suddenly, Dax ripped his lips from mine and looked down at his chest. He touched his skin and looked at me with hurt confusion plastered on his face. "I...I don't understand."

"What's wrong?"

"Rory said when he and Phoenix mated, the wolf symbol appeared on his chest, showing he was part of the pack. I didn't get one. Did it not work? Did I do something wrong?"

"Shh, it's okay," I soothed, combing my fingers through his hair. "Nothing's wrong, cookie. I'm sorry there was a misunderstanding. Our mating linked the two of us to each *other*; it didn't link you to the pack." His eyes narrowed and I explained quickly, "Rory's symbol appeared with his and Phoenix's mating because Phoenix is the Alpha to this pack. He has final decision over his members, so of course his mate was automatically granted rights into the group. If Stone or I would have disputed Rory, we would have been expelled from the pack or killed. The only other way someone is instantly a part of the pack is if they are born into it or if they mate with the Alpha. Otherwise, each potential pack member must be accepted by the others, as well as the Alpha."

"Oh god." Dax's face grew pale. "So they didn't accept me?"

"I'm doing a terrible job of explaining this. I'm so sorry." I paused to kiss his cheek. "There will be a ceremony in which I will present you to the pack as my bonded mate. Each member will give their verdict, and if there is a unanimous acceptance vote, you will be a part of our pack."

"And what happens if there isn't a unanimous vote?"

"You don't need to worry about that. This is all just a formality. Rory loves you and Phoenix is wrapped around his little finger. He'd never go against his mate. And Stone likes you too; he said so."

Dax swallowed hard. "Let's just say for argument's sake that someone votes against me. What would happen?"

"You and I would leave and seek membership within another pack."

"Shit." Anguish danced in my mate's pretty brown eyes. "I can't stand the thought of tearing apart your family."

"The thought isn't worth your worry," I promised before giving his lips a tender peck. "Everything will work out perfectly. And just remember; *you* are the most important person in my life. *You* are my family. I hold you above all others. If my pack does not accept you, I do not accept them. You are my joy and my heart; everything I'll ever need."

"Wow," Dax whispered through trembling lips.

"I'll speak to Phoenix first thing in the morning to take care of this quickly. I don't want you to be troubled. Everything will be okay, my love. We'll always have each other."

Finally he gave me a little smile and nodded. "Will you hold me for a little while?"

"Nothing would make me happier." I laid down beside him and Dax rolled over to rest his cheek on my chest. We were sticky and sweaty, but we'd get cleaned up soon. Right now my mate needed my touch and his needs surpassed everything. I wrapped him in my arms and kissed the top of his head. The feel of his soft, warm body beside me was better than I ever imagined it could be.

Chapter Nine

Dax

"I just...need...a minute," I huffed, leaning against a tree which, thanks to Rowan, I knew was a white oak. We were hiking up a ridiculously steep hill to the site of the ceremony and I was in the driver's seat of the struggle bus. Luckily, Phoenix closed this path to the public until we were finished, so people couldn't witness my difficulty.

I was both relieved and nervous when Rowan spoke with Phoenix early this morning and got the ceremony planned for just a couple of hours later. But now it didn't matter how I felt about the ceremony because I'd never make it anyway. I'd die from exhaustion right here on the path and hikers would just have to step over me because they wouldn't be able to roll my fat ass into the weeds.

"Take your time," Rowan said sweetly, and he massaged my shoulders. My shoulders were fine, though; it was my poor lungs and underused leg muscles that were suffering.

Phoenix and Stone were much further up the path than us, but Rory stayed back with me. Once upon a time, he'd be gasping his last sweet breaths right along with me, but apparently he'd built up his endurance throughout the time he'd spent living in the state park. While I was happy for him, it also made me feel like an even bigger failure. Especially when Phoenix turned around to check on us and Rory waved him on.

"The view from the top is worth it," my bestie promised. "It's beautiful up there. I've gotten so many great pictures of the forest from the trailhead." He smiled dreamily. "Phoenix chose to do this up here because it's actually a pretty special spot. It's where I fell and Phoenix found me;

where he saw me for the first time and knew I was his mate."

"You mean where you nearly fell to your death and smashed your head on a rock? Yes, how romantic," I answered with an eye roll. I couldn't help my sassiness; my lungs burned and my muscles ached. Plus, my breakfast wore off a long time ago and I was getting hangry. Luckily, I didn't offend Rory; he just snorted a laugh and shrugged.

I let out a deep breath. "Okay, I think I can make it a little further." I wasn't sure, but I didn't want to get so far behind Stone and Phoenix that they decided I was dead weight and that they didn't want me bringing down their pack.

"I've got a better idea," Rowan said. He walked in front of me and knelt on one knee, offering me his back. "Climb on."

He didn't have to tell me twice. I snaked my arms around his neck and wrapped my legs around his waist. He stood up, lifting me easily. The man was a beast.

"I brought something for you," Rowan added as he dug in his pocket. My mouth watered at the sound of rustling plastic and I damn near drooled down his neck when he lifted a granola bar into my line of vision. "This trail is long and I wanted to make sure you kept your strength up."

"You're a prince," I replied, snatching the snack as Rowan chuckled and patted my shin. I tried my best not to get crumbs all over him as he carried me the rest of the way up the hill. At my request, he put me down just before we reached Stone and Phoenix. I didn't want them to see that my wolf husband (yes, I totally stole the term from Rory) carried me, though they probably figured it out since the trip didn't take me all damn day.

Rory was right about the view. Stone and Phoenix stood with their backs facing the guardrail, and beyond them were rolling hills covered in trees. Some colorful leaves still clung to them, though they were mostly bare. I couldn't wait to see the scenery next autumn before the leaves fell. That is, if these guys decided to keep me around.

I swallowed hard as Rory took his place between Stone and Phoenix, facing me. Rowan stood beside me and took my hand. He squeezed it in support and I squeezed right back.

"Alpha Phoenix," Rowan began, "Dax and I were paired by Fate and have bonded our bodies and lives together. I present him to you for acceptance into the Pine Ridge Pack."

Phoenix bowed his head at Rowan before turning his attention to me. "It makes my heart glad that the two of you found each other. Rowan has waited nearly eighty years to meet his fated match."

Damn. I never thought to ask how old Rowan was, but it didn't matter; I loved him for his soul, not his age. Besides, eighty years was just a blink when compared to eternity.

"Having found my own mate, I know the deep love that you two share. I know the joy you feel about finding the second half of yourself, and that makes me happy beyond measure. There is nothing greater that I could wish for my friends."

I smiled at Phoenix's sweet words; not only because they confirmed how strongly he felt about Rory, but because he referred to me as his friend. I was proud to call *all* of the men standing here my friends. I felt close to them all and knew we'd only grow closer over time.

"However," Phoenix continued, "Being a part of a pack goes beyond friendship or the bond you share with your mate. If you become a member, Stone, Rory and I will be your brothers. We, along with Rowan, will always fight for you and protect you. We will watch over you for all time, and we expect the same from you in return. Are you prepared to fight for your brothers? To protect this pack until your dying breath?"

"I am," I announced proudly. "I think we've all witnessed today that I'm certainly not the strongest man in this group, but I will do everything I can to protect you all. You three are extremely important to Rowan; you are his family and I want you as my family as well. I would be honored to call you my brothers, and pledge my loyalty to you."

Phoenix and Rory beamed at my words, and Stone gave a nod of his head. Rowan squeezed my hand again, and when I looked up at him, I saw pride shining in his eyes.

"I brought you here for an important reason," Phoenix resumed while waving to the scenery behind him. "Not only does this location hold a special place in my heart, but you can see the beauty of the land here. We're charged with the care and upkeep of the trails. It is our pack's duty to look after these lands and its visitors. Will you do your part by honoring Mother Earth?"

"I will. I'll do everything I can to help if you need me. Plus, Rowan is teaching me about plants and animals around here. The more I learn, the better I can care for the earth."

Phoenix smiled again and looked over at his large friend. "Stone, will you step forward?" *Oh great, start with the wildcard.* Stone did as he was asked. "Given Dax's pledge of protection and loyalty, do you accept him into our pack?"

Stone smirked at me. "When you showed up the other day and saw Phoenix in wolf form, your first instinct was to protect those around you. I think you're stronger than you give yourself credit for. I'm proud to have you as a packmate and brother."

I released a breath I didn't know I was holding. I dropped Rowan's hand and took a step toward Stone, but stopped when he tipped his head in confusion. "Oh...sorry. I was going to hug you, but..." my words died in my throat. Stone surprised me by letting out a booming laugh and wrapping his arms around my shoulders. After a good squeeze, he let me go and I returned to a grinning Rowan.

"Rory, will you please step forward?" Phoenix asked. Rory smiled and approached until he was toe to toe with me. "Do you accept Dax into-"

"Yes," Rory interrupted and the others chuckled. "Dax, you've been my brother for as long as I can remember. You stood by me and looked out for me when I had no one else." He slammed into me and I folded my arms around his middle. "I'm so thankful I get to have you by my side forever. I love you, Dax."

"Love you too, Roar," I whispered. We held each other until Rowan stepped closer to me and put a hand on my back, and Phoenix did the same to Rory. Even though our men knew the love between us wasn't romantic, they were still territorial and I ate that shit right up.

Once Rory and I separated and our husbands each had us tucked securely under their arms (and Stone gave a good eye roll), Phoenix regarded me again. "Dax, the group has voted unanimously, and it is my great pleasure to accept you into the Pine Ridge Pack. As your Alpha, I will guide and protect you for all time. I ask that you now show your allegiance and consent to my leadership."

I blinked at him; I was willing to do whatever he wanted, but was unsure of what the hell I was supposed to do. Stone cleared his throat to get my attention and leaned his head to the side, exposing his neck. I did the same, showing off the mating mark Rowan gave me.

Phoenix tapped two fingers to the side of my throat and the group broke out into applause. *Is that it? Is that what all the fuss was about?* Rowan stepped in front of me and undid the top three buttons of my flannel shirt.

"Oh shit," I whispered to him, "Is this some kind of mating ritual or something? Because I can't do it in front of people." Stone and Phoenix laughed and I remembered (too late) how good shifter hearing was.

"No, cookie. I don't want anyone else to see your beautiful body." *Oh, thank god.* Rowan winked and popped the top few buttons of his shirt as well before spreading the fabric apart, exposing his chest. "Watch."

I gasped when his wolf tattoo became enveloped in a soft golden glow. The light arced from his chest to mine and my skin warmed at the contact. A single black line appeared on my skin. It was still for a moment before bursting apart. What looked like ink spread in every direction, twisting and curling until I had an identical tribal wolf tattoo scripted over my heart. The light died away and I shivered from the loss of its warmth.

"I got a magic tattoo," I whispered to Rowan, who beamed from ear to ear. I turned to a smiling Rory and repeated louder, "I got a magic tattoo!" My friend nodded wildly and ran to me, taking me in his arms. Rowan plastered himself against my back and Phoenix and Stone joined in our huddle as well. We were five grown ass men, group hugging like our lives depended on it.

"Thank you for accepting me," I told them all. "The family I was born into didn't want me, but I've found my *true* family now. I'm pretty sure this is the best day of my life."

Everyone gave me a final squeeze and stepped away, except for Rowan, who wrapped his arms around my waist from behind and nuzzled my neck.

"If everybody wants to come to our place, I'll make lunch," Rory offered. "Plus, I baked a red velvet cake to celebrate; it's Dax's favorite."

My chest warmed again, this time from the love and happiness inside it. Behind me was my eternally bonded wolf husband, before me was my best friend in the world, and around me was my forever family. *And there was cake.* This was *definitely* the best day of my life.

Chapter Ten

Dax

"Are you sure you want to do this?" I asked Rowan from the passenger seat of my car. He was driving me into town to my night shift job of cleaning office buildings. Thankfully it wouldn't be my job much longer. After the pack celebrated together with lunch and cake, Rowan took me back to our home and made sweet love to me. Then we cuddled up together and had a long discussion about our goals and dreams.

Rowan's dream was to of course continue with his work for the pack in taking care of the land and protecting his home and family. But he also wanted to take care of me. He said that if I chose not to work, he'd love to support me financially; it was in a shifter's nature to want to provide for their mate. However, he said he'd also support my decision to work if that's what I wanted; he just asked that I chose a job I enjoyed. He wanted me to be happy in all that I did.

As shocking as it may be, peddling candy at the theater and scrubbing toilets at the office buildings weren't my dream jobs. Not that they were *bad* jobs; they'd provided for me when I needed it. Plus, they were necessary; the world needed careers and workers of all types to continue to function. I was thankful for them and everyone who worked jobs like them, but the work didn't fulfill me personally. The thing is, I didn't know what *would* fulfill me. I'd been so busy trying to make a living for myself and Justin that I never had the time to think about what I wanted out of life.

But thanks to Rowan, I now had time to figure it out. I decided to quit my jobs to spend time with my husband, and to learn about the land and what I could do to help my pack. I also wanted time to get to know Phoenix and Stone better. Plus, Stone promised to teach me how to fight, so that would be an adventure in itself. Then, once I had direction and desire, I'd find a career that spoke to me.

When I called my boss at the movie theater, he said I didn't have to give notice and that I was already written off the schedule. He'd been filling my shifts anyway from where I was ill, and he had plenty of other employees who wanted more hours. My office cleaning boss, however, said she really needed me to work tonight. Another lady called in sick and if I didn't go in, my boss would be stuck cleaning two buildings by herself, which wasn't fair to her.

Rowan volunteered to not only drive me to work, but to stay and help me with the cleaning. The man was a gift, but I felt a little guilty, which explains my original question to him.

"Of course I'm sure," he smiled. I knew being apart from me would hurt him physically, but I was touched that he planned on helping me out. "Besides, we'll make it fun together." I shook my head; sometimes it was hard to believe Rowan was even real, let alone mine.

He parked the car in the abandoned lot in front of the building, making sure to stop under a streetlight. Rowan stood guard over me as I unlocked the door. As soon as we both slipped inside, he quickly locked the entrance behind us. I punched in the security code, retrieved the cleaning supplies from a closet, and we got to work.

And Rowan was right; we made it fun. While we went from room to room vacuuming, gathering trash and sanitizing surfaces, I blasted music from my phone and we danced our asses off. Rowan's moves were clunky and terrible and the most adorable fucking thing I'd ever seen. We stopped cleaning for a makeout session after he caught sight of me shaking my ass while bending over to pick something up off of the floor.

When it was time to clean the restrooms, Rowan cracked me up by making a makeshift hazmat suit out of trash bags. He ripped two holes in the bottom of one to stick his legs through and cinched the drawstring around his waist. Then he made holes for his head and arms in another one and pulled it on like a t-shirt. He was the only man alive who could still look sexy while wearing garbage bags. When I told him that, we made out again.

He insisted on scrubbing the toilets while I cleaned the mirrors. When we were done, we sprayed each other down with disinfectant like it was fancy cologne as I doubled over with laughter. It didn't matter what we did together, Rowan made it enjoyable. He was weird and wonderful and perfect for me. He was the only person on Earth who could give me the time of my life while cleaning.

Four hours, two stories, and three makeout sessions later, we finished with our work. We carried all the bags of garbage as well as recycling down to the back door of the ground level.

"I can take the recycling out to the bins if you want to carry the garbage to the compactor," I offered.

"Are they close to each other?"

I shook my head no. "The trash compactor is around the back corner and the recycling bins are up towards the front door."

"I'll take them both," he insisted. "I want you to stay inside, okay?" I nodded and my heart warmed at how protective he was over me. Rowan gathered up all of the bags, gave me a quick kiss and stepped outside into the dark night.

Just a minute later, the door pushed open. I'd left it unlocked and propped open so Rowan could get back in easily and we could head home. "You're back already? I thought you'd be gone for-" I stopped talking when a figure entered and I saw that it wasn't Rowan. "Justin? What the hell are you doing here?"

Anger flashed across his face at my words but he quickly schooled his expression. "I've come here every night looking for you since you left, sweetie pie." *Oh god, he's laying it on thick*. The cutesy name I always longed to hear now made my stomach churn. "You left me no choice. You haven't answered any of my calls or texts." Thankfully I didn't get cell service in the state park, so I didn't even know he'd tried contacting me. I would have ignored him even if I did.

"I was waiting across the street and saw you arrive with that other man," Justin explained. "I was watching the doors and waited until he left and I knew I could talk to you alone." He was probably scared to death of my strong man. Good call.

"Why, so you could use me as your punching bag again?" I snipped, propping a hand on my hip.

Justin's jaw clenched before he took a deep breath to calm himself down. "Look, I'm sorry about what happened between us. It's just...you went back on your deal and I got angry. But I've forgiven you, and I'll even overlook the stunt you pulled with the food on the floor because I miss you. Now that you're feeling better, you can come home and things can go back to normal."

"Pass," I shrugged, and his eyes widened. "Justin, you and I both know that you're not sorry about shit. You're here because you haven't had someone to cook for you and clean up after you. You don't miss me; you miss my services. You thought you could sweet talk me into coming back, but it's not gonna happen. It took me too fucking long, but now I know I deserve better than you."

"Listen here, you fat shit-"

"Oh, *there's* the real Justin," I interrupted with a smirk. "I was wondering when you'd show up."

"You need to watch your mouth," Justin growled. "You should be grateful for the chance to cook for me and clean up after me. It's better than your fat ass deserves." He really needed to get some new material. "I'm the best you're ever gonna get."

"Yeeaaah, that's where you're wrong," I replied with a fake look of pity. "Not only are you the worst fucking person I can think of, I found an amazing man. He thinks I'm beautiful and funny and he loves me for who I am, not what I can do for him."

"You're a lying sack of shit," he snarled angrily, spraying me down with saliva.

"Okay, first of all, *gross*," I replied, wiping a hand across my face. "And secondly, no, I'm not lying." I pushed my bottom lip out again. "I guess you'll have to be a big boy and learn how to pick up your own mess." A week ago, I wouldn't have dreamed of speaking to Justin like this. But I was stronger now, and I knew how terrible he truly was.

That still didn't mean it was the greatest idea. Justin pushed me against the wall and cocked his fist back. "I guess you didn't learn your lesson the first time." I scrunched my eyes closed, waiting for the blow to come.

When it didn't, I peeled my eyelids open to find Rowan's hand wrapped around Justin's fist, and my lover glaring fire at my ex. His expression softened when he turned to me. "Are you hurt?" Even before taking care of business with Justin, his first priority was caring for me. I quickly shook my head no.

"Who the fuck are you?" Justin asked Rowan. His voice was strained, surely from the pain of my lover squeezing his hand. He should consider himself lucky that Rowan was holding himself back; he could pulverize Justin's bones if he so chose.

"He's my husband, asshole," I replied with a proud smirk.

"Bullshit. Someone like him wouldn't want some-" Justin's words cut out when Rowan wrapped his hand around his throat. He slammed Justin's back against the wall and got within an inch of his face.

"You listen to me," Rowan growled. His voice was different than I'd ever heard it; low, raspy and menacing. Not gonna lie; my dick did a little wiggle of approval in my jeans. "You've mistreated Dax for far too long, and I will not allow it to continue. You don't deserve your next breath, but I won't subject my sweet husband to witnessing your death. But know this; if you *ever* try to contact him again, I *will* kill you, and I won't make it quick or painless. Do you understand?"

Justin nodded and Rowan sniffed the air. He looked down and I followed his gaze to see a large dark spot growing in my ex's jeans. *Holy shit, he pissed himself. This day just keeps getting better.* I snorted a laugh and Rowan winked at me before turning back to Justin.

"Go." He released his hand and Justin's ass hit the floor hard. He scrambled to his feet and he disappeared out the back door. Rowan kicked the door shut, locked it, and turned to me. "Are you okay?"

"Thanks to you." I snuggled up to him and Rowan wrapped his arms tightly around my shoulders. He kissed the top of my head and took a deep whiff of my hair.

"I never dreamed he'd show up like this. I'm sorry that I left you alone. I thought I was keeping you safe but I put you in harm's way and-"

"Hey," I interrupted, looking up at him with a smile. "I never dreamed he'd show up either. And you *did* keep me safe. Who knows what he would have done to me if you hadn't stopped him? You protected me, Row."

"I'll always protect you."

"I know you will." I lurched up on my tiptoes for a kiss. "I love you."

"I love you too. Now let's get out of this hallway; it smells like piss."

I laughed and took his hand as we rounded the corner. I couldn't smell anything, but his enhanced senses were probably going crazy.

I tucked the cleaning supplies away, set the alarm and locked the door as we stepped outside again. The night was cold, so Rowan tucked me under his arm to keep me as warm as possible as we walked to my car.

Rowan shook his head and twitched his nose. "I can't get rid of his stench," he explained when I gave him a funny look. "It's almost like he's still-"

The words were barely passed his lips when Justin jumped out from around the front of my car and, too quickly for us to process what was happening, plunged a knife into Rowan's chest. I screamed and

Justin erupted into maniacal laughter. His eyes were wild and unfocused; he looked truly unhinged.

"Not so tough now, are you?" Justin taunted. He must have been too afraid to use his weapon when Rowan had the upper hand, but decided to use the element of surprise.

"Oh my god, Row, are you okay?" I asked as I patted my hands all over his chest, which was wet with fresh blood and heaved with ragged breaths. Rowan stumbled backwards and leaned against the side of my car.

Tears welled up in my eyes when I remembered Rory's words; '*The only way they can die is if you like, stab them in the heart or cut off their head or something*'. "Please don't leave me. You're so strong. I know you can get through this. Please, Row; *please* don't go."

"It's no use," Justin said with a wicked smile. "You get to watch him die and then I'll carve your fat ass up. That will teach you to laugh at me." Little did he know if Rowan died, I would too and Justin wouldn't get the pleasure of killing me. *Somehow* that silver lining didn't cheer me up.

I slipped my hand into my husband's. "Stay with me," I begged Rowan, ignoring Justin. I'd likely be dead in a few minutes and I didn't want to spend any of that time on him. "I've still got flowers to learn, and so many naughty firsts to show you. I want forever with you."

Rowan squeezed my hand as his breathing slowly evened out. He leaned down to kiss my cheek and whispered in my ear, "I'm okay, my love. He missed." He clutched the handle of the knife and pulled it from his chest as Justin's eyes widened with confusion and fear. Tears of happiness flooded my cheeks as I watched Rowan's wound seal closed between the shredded fabric of his shirt.

I hastily dried my face so that I could clearly see Justin's terrified expression. "Oh, you are *so* fucked."

Justin turned tail and tried to run away, but Rowan caught him by the back of the neck. He dragged my ex around the back of the building while he begged for mercy. I trailed behind them, praying Rowan didn't give it to him. I wasn't a vengeful person necessarily, but seeing Justin attack my husband lit a hatred and need for revenge inside me that I didn't know I was capable of.

But it was more than that. What if Rowan *did* let him go? I'd spend the rest of my life looking over my shoulder, wondering if he was coming for me. He wanted to kill me tonight; Rowan too. Why would I think he'd stop trying? Even if he did, I knew he'd move on to the next poor man and treat him as badly as he treated me. He'd use him, possibly abuse him...or worse. He tried to kill tonight. I believed with everything in me he'd try again.

"Please," Justin begged when Rowan came to a stop next to the trash compactor. "Don't do this. You're okay, Dax is okay...just let me go and I'll never bother you again, just like you wanted."

"I gave you that chance and you blew it," Rowan muttered. "You threatened to kill my mate and now you *dare* ask for forgiveness?"

Seeing he was unswayed, Justin turned to me. "We had some good times, didn't we? You loved me once. Don't let him do this."

"You just tried to kill my husband," I reminded him. "You really don't want me on your jury right now."

"No, no, no," Justin argued quickly. "You're too nice to kill me; too sweet. If you do this, you'll never get over it. It will haunt your dreams forever."

"Which is why *I'm* going to do it," Rowan interjected. "I've killed before and I sleep just fine." *That was the most badass statement I've ever heard.* Rowan got my attention with a serious expression. "Look away, cookie."

I did as he asked because I knew Justin was right. Seeing his demise would haunt my dreams, no matter how much I hated him or he deserved to die.

"No, please, I'll do anything you-" I flinched when Justin's words were cut off by the unmistakable sound of a blade piercing skin, which was followed by gurgled moans. Feet shuffled and dragged against the pavement before metal clanged against metal.

A motor whirred and hydraulics hissed. More moans and then shrieks of agony accompanied the sound of bones snapping and organs smashing. I could have covered my ears at any point, but a sick part of me wanted - *needed* to hear it.

And then...nothing. The motor fell silent. The moans stopped. Silence settled over me and somehow made me more uncomfortable than what I just heard. I flinched again when something touched my shoulder, but I relaxed when I opened my eyes to find Rowan's arm around me.

Rowan wiped Justin's blade clean on his jeans, leaving red streaks on the denim before tucking the knife into his pocket.

"Come on," Rowan said with a gentle squeeze to my shoulder, "Let's get you home."

Chapter Eleven

Rowan

The drive home was filled with silence. I worried my sweet mate was overwhelmed by the events of the evening, so I didn't press for him to speak. I gave him space but I would be there for him whenever he needed me.

I hated that Dax was burdened, but I had no remorse for what I did. Justin made an attempt on my life and threatened to do the same to Dax. *No one* threatened my mate as long as I had air in my lungs.

I parked in front of our cabin and helped Dax inside. "Cookie, I need to go speak with Stone for a few minutes. Why don't you take a nice hot shower to relax? I'll be home as soon as I can."

Dax nodded and shuffled off to the bathroom without a word. My heart ached for him. My mate was too sweet to endure what happened. I should have done a better job of protecting him from it, but in the moment, I needed him close to me. I needed my eyes on him to know he was safe. I promised myself I'd do whatever I could to make it up to him when I got home.

I ran to Stone's place and knocked on his door. I breathed a sigh of relief when he answered quickly.

"Jesus, what happened to you?" he asked, looking at my bloodstained clothing with wide eyes. His eyes only grew wider (though it was from excitement) as I told him about the events of the night. "Holy shit, you put him in a trash compactor? That's incredible! Did you record it?"

I narrowed my eyes at him. "No, I didn't record it!"

"Damn. Well, why didn't you call me? I would've loved to watch that!"

His enthusiasm didn't surprise me. "Sorry, it was kind of a spur of the moment decision. Anyway, I need your help."

He stood straighter and the amusement left his face. "What can I do?" He was always happy to help his pack when they were in need.

"I brought the knife home with me so I didn't leave a weapon with fingerprints at the scene, but, well, as you can imagine, Justin's death was a bit...messy." His grin returned. "And I needed to get Dax away from there quickly before he saw."

"Shit, I bet the poor guy is freaked the hell out."

I nodded with a sad smile. "I need to be with him now, but the scene needs to be cleaned up. I checked and there are no security cameras around the parking lot or building, so nothing was caught on film. But if someone finds Justin's body, I don't want Dax involved in this. He lived with the man and had a relationship with him; he'll be the first person to pop up in an investigation."

I knew from Rory that Justin never let Dax post any pictures or information about them on social media and never went out into public with him (the bastard), but he still received mail at the home they shared and I didn't want my love to get into any kind of trouble.

"So you need me to retrieve the body...or rather, what's left of it, and bleach away any DNA and signs Justin was ever there in the first place," Stone surmised. I nodded and he sighed. "Dammit, do you know how much trash I'm going to have to sift through to make sure I get all of his pieces out?"

"I'm sorry," I told him honestly. In retrospect, a trash compactor probably wasn't the best way to kill a man. "I owe you one."

"No you don't," he insisted. "You did what you needed to for your mate and I'm happy to help. You go take care of Dax and I'll fill Phoenix in on what happened. I'm sure he'll help out and we'll get it done quickly."

"Thank you, Stone." I gave him a quick hug of appreciation. "Please tell Rory that I know he'll want to comfort Dax, but I need to be alone with him now. I'll have him call or visit when he's feeling up to it."

"Can do." He huffed a laugh. "He'll probably want to throw you a parade for killing that bastard."

"Tell him no parade necessary, but I wouldn't turn down a batch of snickerdoodles for my mate."

He laughed again. "Good lord, you're whipped. Okay, go look after your man and I'll take care of everything." I thanked him again and jogged across the clearing to my home.

When I entered, I found Dax in the bedroom stepping into a pair of sleep pants. His skin was pink from his hot shower and water droplets clung to his hair. He was so beautiful and all I wanted to do was take him into my arms and love on him, but first I needed to scrub Justin's pungent scent from my skin.

I took a shower in the hottest water I could stand and cleansed my body three times until his odor no longer lingered on it. I dried off and wrapped a towel around my waist to wear into the bedroom.

Dax was sitting on the edge of the mattress with his feet on the floor. He knotted his fingers in front of him and his uneasy expression broke my heart. I slowly sat down next to him so I wouldn't startle him and draped my arm across his shoulders.

"What's wrong, my love?" I wanted him to unload his burdens onto me and let me carry them for him.

"I'm scared," he admitted quietly.

"I'm so sorry. I never meant to frighten you. I should have-"

"Done exactly what you did," he finished, placing his hand on my thigh. "Row, I'm not scared of you or because of you...I'm scared *for* you. I know why you did what you did and I'll fight to defend you in every way I can, but others may not feel the same way. Someone's going to find him and the cops will get involved and I'm afraid they'll take you away from me." He looked up at me with watery eyes. "I can't lose you."

"Oh, Dax." I tightened my hold on him and thanked Fate for such a sweet and wonderful man. "Nothing will ever take me away from you."

"But what if-"

I quieted him with a kiss to his lips. "Rid your worries from your mind. I spoke with Stone and he and Phoenix are going to use the night cover to clear away all evidence that *any* of us were there tonight."

"And...Justin's body?"

"Will go where no one will ever find it." Dax breathed a sigh of relief. "That's what a pack is for, remember? We'll always look out for each other. Was that the only thing bothering you?"

"Yeah," he replied with a nod. "Maybe it's super fucked up that I'm not more compassionate, but all of my compassion went out the window when he stabbed you. He could have killed you, Row; he could have killed both of us."

"But we're still here," I replied gently. "Don't worry yourself with the 'what ifs' or 'could have beens'. Focus on the here and now and how lucky we are to have each other."

"We *are* lucky," he agreed, finally giving me a little smile. "*I'm* lucky. You know, when I told Justin he was fucked, it wasn't because I thought you'd get revenge for yourself, but because you'd make him pay for threatening me and hitting me in the past. I knew you would do anything to protect my honor and keep me safe."

"Of course I would, and I always will," I promised. "I'm just relieved you weren't scared of my reaction to him."

"Rowan, you are the sweetest man I've ever met. You'd never hurt someone just for the fun of it. I know as a shifter you have an aggressive side, but I also know that I don't need to be afraid of it. I think you'd rather chop your balls off than hurt me." I enthusiastically nodded my agreement. A man shouldn't be so eager when speaking about castrating himself, but that's how much I loved Dax.

"And...can I tell you a secret?" Dax asked as he rubbed his hand up and down my thigh. I swallowed hard and gave him a nod. "It was incredibly sexy to see you get so worked up over me."

"Yeah?" I asked in a husky voice.

"Oh yeah." He caressed higher up on my thigh and my towel got a little tighter. "I love when you're my sweetheart, but also when you're kicking ass for me." He caressed over the growing lump in my towel and I gave a throaty moan. "It was so hot seeing my man's strength and wild side; I want you to show me more."

"How?" I doubted I could do much more damage to Justin's body, but I'd certainly try if it made him happy.

Dax answered by unwrapping the towel from around my waist, exposing my hard cock to the air. He tickled up my heated flesh and looked at me with fire in his eyes. "With this."

Ohhh. It took me entirely too long to catch on, but in my defense, I'd always thought of making love to Dax as an intimate, sensual experience. But if Dax wanted me to let a little of my wild side out, I was happy to give my mate anything he needed.

I trailed my hand up his hairy belly and chest, and Dax hummed when I flicked my thumb across his nipple. "You want me to take control of your beautiful body and make you feel so good?"

"Yes. I want to see raw and primal Rowan. Remind me who I belong to." He knew I didn't own him; he was my bonded mate to keep by my side and love forever. I belonged to him too. But he wanted intense and passionate, and his words lit my blood on fire.

I stood from the bed and flung my damp towel to the other side of the room. I took Dax's hands and pulled him to his feet. With a single tug, his cotton sleep pants pooled around his feet on the floor. His cock was at half-mast and filling quickly.

Dax's lips parted and the tip of his tongue swept between them, making them glisten. His fingers twitched at his side with the need to touch. But he didn't move towards me; he simply tipped his head to the side, exposing the pretty mating mark on his throat. Whether subconscious or intended, it was an unmistakable sign of submission.

I stepped forward and crashed our lips together. I cradled the back of his head in both hands and dominated his mouth, licking and nipping while Dax moaned and let me take control. I captured his bottom lip between my teeth and pulled back before releasing it with a snap.

"Holy shit," Dax whispered breathlessly. "That was so hot."

I was just getting started. My wolf side loved that I was taking the reins and my human side loved that my mate was enjoying himself. It made my pulse race and my body ache for more.

"Climb up onto the bed on your hands and knees."

Dax spun around and did as I asked, exposing himself fully to me. I lowered myself onto my knees and took a moment to appreciate the breathtaking sight before me. His balls hung heavy between his thighs, nestled against his cock which was now hard and leaking. His pretty pink hole quivered in anticipation.

I didn't make him wait. I palmed his fleshy mounds, spread them apart, and dove in, touching my tongue to his pucker.

"Ohhh god," Dax moaned. "Please, Row; more."

I flattened my tongue and licked against him, tasting his sweet flesh and a subtle hint of soap. I trailed around his rim, loving the way each ridge tickled against my taste buds. Dax whimpered as I devoured his delicious little hole. I licked and lapped, nipped and sucked until he was writhing beneath me.

He whimpered again when I removed my tongue, but I wasn't done with him yet. I placed a line of wet kisses down his taint and onto his balls. I ran my tongue along their fuzzy surface and sucked each one gingerly into my mouth. I laved them until they were soaked and Dax was breathless.

I quickly grabbed the lube from my bedside table. I drenched my cock and two fingers, which I pressed to Dax's hole.

"Don't prep me," he requested. "I'm so close already. I just want you to take me; stretch me open with your huge dick."

Shit. I took a deep breath to keep myself from passing out at Dax's sexy words. I moved my hands to grip Dax's curvy, padded hips and lined my tip up with his entrance.

Slowly and gently, I pressed forward as Dax cried out into the room. I sank every inch of my cock into his warm, tight ass until my pubes bumped his skin.

"Fuck me, Row!" Dax pleaded in a strangled cry.

I pulsed my hips back and forth and my eyes nearly crossed from pleasure. The heat and grip of his body were perfection. His walls squeezed my flesh and lights burst behind my eyes every time our balls kissed together.

I wasn't going to last. I dipped my right hand beneath him and curled it around his cock, which was soaked with pre-cum. I stroked him wildly while I fucked him the same way. I planted my feet on the floor and slammed my weight into him, burying my cock inside him while he begged for more.

Suddenly, Dax's body tensed beneath me. His knuckles went white as he gripped the blankets beside him. He screamed my name and his dick pulsed in my hand. Warm cum spilled from him and covered my fingers.

His ass clenched around my cock in time with the throbbing of his dick, kneading and milking my length. My balls lifted and rolled. I slammed into my lover and my orgasm ripped through me with such strength it made my head spin. I poured burst after burst of my seed into Dax, filling him to the brim.

Neither of us said a word as we fought to catch our breath. It took several minutes for my heart to stop pounding in my ears. I eased my softening dick from his body and massaged his well-loved hole with my fingers, hoping to ease away any soreness.

Dax hummed happily and rested his cheek on the mattress. "That was amazing."

"It's always amazing," I countered before leaning over to press open mouthed kisses down his spine.

"Mm, you're so right. I love when you're gentle and tender, and when you're rough and nasty." I chuckled against his back. "Does my sweetheart Rowan want to cuddle?"

"Cookie, you *never* have to ask me that."

He laughed as he climbed to the top of the bed and burrowed under the covers. I wiped my cum-coated hand on my discarded towel before joining him, and Dax wasted no time in snuggling up against me and resting his head on my chest. I wrapped my arms around him and let out a happy sigh.

"I love you, Rowan," Dax whispered as he nuzzled deeper into me. "For your sweetness *and* your strength. For the way you keep me safe and the way you make me laugh. You make me feel like I'm not only good enough, but that you're blessed to have me."

His sweet words melted my heart. "I *am* blessed to have you, Dax. I'll never take a day with my perfect mate for granted, and I promise to spend forever showing you how much I love you."

Dax raised his head for a kiss before he snuggled down again. I tucked the blankets around him to make sure he was warm enough and caressed my hand up and down his back. Before long, my beautiful man relaxed against me and his breathing turned slow and deep.

*****

A gentle knock roused me from sleep. Light spilled in around the drapes over my windows and a peek at the clock told me it was the first light of dawn. Dax was still snoozing soundly against me, so I eased out of bed gently so I wouldn't wake him up. I stepped into a pair of sweatpants before answering the front door, finding Stone, Phoenix and Rory on my porch.

"It took a while, but it's done," Stone informed me as a greeting. "Phoenix and I gathered up all of Justin's bits and pieces and bleached the shit out of that place. No one will ever know he was there, and no one will ever find his remains."

"He's triple bagged and buried deep in the earth," Phoenix added. "In a part of the forest inaccessible to humans."

"Thank you both so much," I offered sincerely, and they bowed their heads to me.

"How is Dax doing?" Rory asked. "When he didn't call last night, I figured he was pretty upset. I made him these." He lifted a platter full of snickerdoodles and a bolt of guilt shot through me.

"He's actually doing really well. He's sleeping right now. I'm sorry he didn't call you; we were...busy last night and then he fell asleep."

"Busy, huh?" Stone asked with a smirk. "Damn, he got over that pretty quick."

"Aw, there's lots of dick healing around this place," Rory said. Phoenix snickered and nodded his agreement, but I gave him a look of confusion.

"I don't get it," Stone stated and I was glad I wasn't the only one.

"Nevermind," Rory replied with a wave of his hand. "I just meant I get where Dax is coming from; he finally had a man fighting *for* him for a change and I can see where that'd get his blood pumping. Besides, I know how hot it is to see your mate in action." Phoenix gave him a smile and leaned in for a kiss.

"Well, I guess that means Dax won't be needing these," Stone insisted, grabbing the platter of cookies.

"Excuse you, those are for my mate." I swatted his hand away, but as I grabbed the plate, Stone snatched a cookie and shoved it in his mouth unapologetically. I glared at him, but Phoenix spoke up and got my attention.

"I'm happy to hear your mate is doing well. I'm going to go catch up on some sleep myself."

"Thank you again, Alpha; you too, Stone." They bowed their heads again and Stone stole another cookie.

"Have Dax come over when he gets up," Rory requested. "I want to talk to him about everything."

"I will." It made me happy that my mate had such a good friend in Rory.

Everyone bid me goodbye and walked away to their respective cabins. I retreated back inside and placed the snickerdoodles on the counter. Since it was officially morning, I decided I would surprise my mate with breakfast in bed. I smiled as I pulled the skillet out of the cabinet; I couldn't wait to spend the rest of time spoiling my beloved mate.

Thank you for reading *Mine to Keep*! If you enjoyed the book, please consider leaving a review. Stay tuned for the third and final book in the *Pine Ridge Pack* series, *Mine to Protect*, which features Stone's book, coming soon!

<u>Other Reads (Free with Kindle Unlimited):</u>

<u>M/M Paranormal Romance:</u>

Once Bitten: Javier Coven Book 1 (Vampire M/M)

Twice Shy: Javier Coven Book 2
(Vampire M/M)

Twice Bitten: Javier Coven Book 3
(Vampire M/M/M)

Untitled: Duff Coven Book 1 (Vampire
M/M) Coming soon!

Mine to Save: Pine Ridge Pack Book 1
(M/M Wolf Shifter)

Mine to Keep: Pine Ridge Pack Book 2
(M/M Wolf Shifter)

Mine to Protect: Pine Ridge Pack Book 3
(M/M Wolf Shifter) Coming soon!

Shadow Walker: Bay City Coven Book 1
(Vampire M/M)

Into the Shadows: Bay City Coven Book
2 (Vampire M/M) Coming soon!

Magic Touch (M/M Mage)

M/M Series:

Arrested Hearts Book 1: Gage & Tyson (M/M) *Can be read as standalone

Arrested Hearts Book 2: Chris & Lyle (M/M)

Arrested Hearts Book 3: Mike & Jonah (M/M)

Arrested Hearts Book 4: Sam & Jordan (M/M) Coming soon!

My Everything (M/M) *Can be read as standalone

My Forever (novella sequel to "My Everything") (M/M)

Head Over Wheels (M/M) *Can be read as standalone

Head Over Wheels: Book 2 (M/M)

Care for You (Head Over Wheels: Book 3) (M/M)

My Grumpy Old Bear (Loveable Grumps: Book 1) *Can be read as standalone

My Confused Cub (Lovable Grumps: Book 2) Coming soon!

Beautiful Dreamer (M/M Age Play) (Secret Desires: Book 1) *Can be read as standalone

Lost Boy (M/M BDSM) (Secret Desires: Book 2) Coming soon!

M/M Standalone

Ours to Love (M/M/M)

Chasing Jackson (M/M)

Nervous Nate (M/M Age Play Romance)

Valentine Shmalentine (M/M)

M/F Series:

Housewife Chronicles: Complete Series (M/F)

Luscious: Complete Series (M/F)

Made in the USA
Coppell, TX
22 June 2021